I0710126

ARTIFICIAL

A horror collection by

CW Briar

PLEASE draw on these pages.
Add your own unique contributions.

Every doodle is influenced by centuries of inherited human experience.

Never underestimate the worth of your art.

ISBN: 978-1-964645-00-1

This is a work of fiction. Names, characters, businesses, places, events, and incidents are either the products of the author's imagination or used in a fictional manner. Any resemblance to actual persons, living or dead, or actual events is purely coincidental - I mean, if a very, VERY famous person or place is mentioned in a book like this, then it's probably referring to whom or what you think it is, but we should all know how fiction works by now. This is a work of make-believe. I'm not inventing or hallucinating libelous claims about real people - I'll leave that job to the AIs.

Editing: Angela R. Watts and The Damascus Blades

Cover Art: Trevor Henderson

Interior Art: CW Briar, Lily Wasielewski, and Ava Czekala

This book is dedicated to the genuine artists who have enriched our lives with their talents,

their dedication,

their visions,

their authenticity,

and their souls.

01010011 01110101 01100011 01101011 00100000 01101001 01110100 00101100 00100000 01110010 01101111 01100010 01101111 01110100 00100000 01101111 01110110 01100101 01110010 01101100 01101111 01110010 01100100 01110011 00101110

STORIES

THE ART THIEF

Once upon a time, there was a fair, young maiden with a heart full of colors.

Her parents were jewelers who had moved from a distant kingdom to sell their wares. To fit in with the language of their new home, they named their daughter Gemma, thus foretelling the girl's passion for brilliant colors. As an infant, Gemma would squeal with rapturous delight at the polished stones dangling from her mother's neck and ears. Her fingers were not only inquisitive but quick, and sometimes she would manage to tug an earring. Her mother would gasp in pain and scold baby Gemma, but then she would reassure her with a smile like diamonds.

In school, other children hastily colored their shapes and animals so they could spend all of recess outdoors, but not Gemma. She took her time. Gemma spread rainbows outside the lines, all the way to the pearly edges of the pages. She wore her crayons down until their wrappings were completely gone.

Nature was a feast for young Gemma. During hikes, her eyes would be overfed with so much splendor, she wished they had belts that could be loosened, much like the belt her father loosened after Thanksgiving dinners. She loved the mint and sage of the fields, the jade and umber of the forests, the slate, amethyst, and ivory of the mountains. At the beach, others used sand to build castles, but Gemma let the crystalline grains pour through her fingers so she could study their tiny, infinite hues. She watched with envy as the sun dipped like a brush into the ocean, painting cadmium, fuchsia, and indigo on the emerald waves.

Her classmates called her Rainbow Gemma because she added color to everything. At the grand ball known as the middle school dance, where white princes and princesses swayed together, Gemma danced alone in a dress like a tropical garden. Green hugged her. Purple twirled around her legs. Yellow straps brushed her black hair off her shoulders. When she was thirsty, she hung out at the punchbowl, which had a drink called Orange Kiss.

Gemma's parents recognized her bond with colors was more than infatuation—it was destiny. On her fourteenth birthday, they gave her a ring with marbled hues. It was a bit too large for her finger, and they offered to resize it, but Gemma declined. She enjoyed spinning it, watching the colors turn like a chromatic vortex. Her parents also gave her a set of oil paints. In no time, she was filling canvases to the far, pearly edges with her favorite landscapes. The colors she recreated almost glowed, the paintings seemingly backlit like stained glass at sunrise.

Her parents weren't the only ones to marvel at Gemma's creations. They put the paintings in local galleries and cafes, and crowds formed. People stared at the rectangular forests, mountains, and beaches. They would touch the brush strokes as if doubtful they were real. This had to be the work of a master artisan, not a teenaged girl with a set of oil paints. This was magic on cotton. The paintings sold, and Gemma learned people valued this newfound passion of hers.

***

For a while, Gemma's family was happy. The jewelry store they had built was thriving, but their footing in this foreign kingdom was always weak and slippery. Their success was vulnerable.

For reasons that had nothing to do with Gemma's family, an angry fervor arose in the city. Crowds gathered like sticks in the streets, protests poured out like oil, and riots struck a match. Bricks flew, and one soared through the jewelry store's window. Hammers pummeled metal bars, and throngs of furious people saw green in the shop's multicolored treasure.

Hours later, Gemma's father would arrive to find empty shelves torched with fire and sprayed with paint.

The Fates had made their first cut, but they would not be satisfied until they had sawed to the bone in Gemma's life. Her parents thought they were protected from theft and fire by the contracts they had received and the lines they had signed upon—contracts forged by a business partner more familiar with the rules of this kingdom. The partner had lied, and he fled to lands unknown with what treasure remained. The fire made paupers of the family, and Gemma wept with her parents over the ashes.

They sold possessions one-by-one, including the magnificent, colorful earrings and necklaces that once adorned Gemma's mother—Gemma, however, was allowed to keep her marbled ring. They moved to an apartment where Gemma slept beside her parents, for she no longer had a room of her own. Insects scampered in the shower and under the bed of their new residence. Gemma had hoped to one day have a dog like the children at her old school, but now guns barked in the night instead. She continued to paint until the colors dwindled and eventually ran out. Gemma lacked supplies. The girl whose art outshone rainbows put away her paintbrushes, with all their worn bristles, into a gray box in a gray closet.

Her parents worked wearisome jobs to regain what was lost, but the strain of broken dreams proved too great. Their personalities turned from sweet to rancid like forgotten fruit. Some days they were sad, some days they were angry, and some days they shouted at Gemma or each other for reasons she couldn't understand. Then, one night, her father came home under the dark spell of alcohol and fired one of the barking guns into Gemma, her mother, and himself. Gemma survived, and when the paramedics arrived, they found Gemma lying in a triple pool of crimson, petrified by the red on the gray ceiling, gray floor, and gray walls.

***

A judge imprisoned Gemma with a distant aunt she barely knew. The counterfeit family did not accept her. They pelted her with insults because of the inconvenience she was to them. The children pulled her hair and kicked her shins because she took one of their beds. Along with beans and rice, the aunt served guilt to Gemma at every meal. The sorrow caused her to struggle in school. Soon, she was being bullied by girls who were prettier, richer, and better able to hide their tears.

No wonder, then, Gemma left her aunt's home as soon as she was old enough. She chose the streets, which were equally cruel, but at least they did not know her name. Were her parents alive and their shop still open, Gemma would have been preparing for university, one which could train her to be a masterful artist. Instead, she labored every day to keep a roof over her head and food in her bowl. Jobs came and went. She hated them all, and they hated her in return. She learned to pick locks so she could sleep in garages and storage rooms when she lacked money for rent. Gemma was a young woman who could no longer dream of having dreams.

One day, on a street where broken people slept in alcoves and alleys, Gemma was stopped by something in the window of a pawn shop. There, on top of four canvases, was the prettiest box of paints Gemma had ever seen. The wood grain flowed like a mountain spring, and the colorful circles on the lid reminded her of gems set into gold. The kit contained everything, even paintbrushes. She felt worlds awakening in her hand, begging to be released. Her mind craved the pigments the way an empty stomach craves fresh-baked bread, the way ears crave music in quiet, troubled times.

Gemma had to wait outside the locked door until a buzzer sounded. The shop's sticky floor popped and crackled under her like the spine of an ancient witch. The room smelled of damp, dust, and burnt tobacco. The shopkeeper troll seated behind the counter raised an eyebrow and then raised his baggy posture so he could better see Gemma as she approached. His beard was a graying thicket, and more hair hung from his nostrils than from atop his head.

Gemma hugged her arms across her chest.

Hello, the troll croaked.

Hello, Gemma squeaked.

The wan troll tried to guess what she had come to buy. Was she there for a dress? A necklace? A knife for protection? Every guess was wrong. She knew he was talking to delay her, buying more time to taste her with his bespectacled, reptilian eyes.

When he drew in a phlegmy breath, Gemma asked about the painting set.

The shopkeeper lit a cigar and told a tale of an artist who had died with a needle in her arm. He licked his lips.

Do you want to see it?

He put aside the button that controlled the locked front door and buzzer. The shopkeeper came around the counter and followed her to the window display. His careless lumbering bumped items that hung off the crowded racks. When the shopkeeper laid the treasure in Gemma's hands and opened the lid to reveal everything inside, she knew she had to take it home.

How much?

The shopkeeper gave a price that made Gemma touch the thin, folded bills in her pocket, then she touched her marbled ring. Her cupboards were almost bare, and her landlord had already threatened to take her key if she missed another rent. Gemma bartered, offering a morsel of what the trollish shopkeeper asked for. She was doing him a favor, no? He did not know what he had. There would be space in the window to sell something of even greater value.

He laughed at her offer. She could smell where he had been, how many cigars he had smoked, how long it had been since he labored to wash the tricky parts of his body.

What about that ring?

Gemma turned her ring, testing if it could be removed from her finger. With a hard tug, she could slip it over her knuckle, but she lacked the strength to do so. The pain of trying went up her arm to her heart. She considered more options. Would someone else take the paints if she waited for a day when she had more money? Would there ever *be* a day when she had more money? If she sold the ring, the meaning of its colors would be forgotten by those who saw a mere trinket.

Could I pay more next month?

That's not how this works.

Of course, it wasn't how this worked. There had to be an exchange of what each other wanted. The only other option for Gemma was to leave and hope she had enough coins the next time she found a perfect paint set, but that would have required hope.

She let herself be taken into the back room, which was cluttered with the shopkeeper's hoard. Everything was covered with the grime of dead hopes. He locked the door and cleared a space on the table, one under the vulturous eye of a security camera. Gemma held onto her ring as she let her garments be unfastened. The musk of the troll's desperation turned her stomach, but she surrendered.

It was clear by how the shopkeeper moved he had not scraped his tumbleweed scruff against the cheek of a woman in a long, long time. He panted like an ox pulling a wagon through mud. His bulk climbed Gemma and beat upon her, and she endured with clenched fists, waiting for her chance to hold the paints again. She paid for the treasure with interest, and the only mercy the shopkeeper gave was in letting her take the four canvases along with the box.

The air in that neighborhood had never been clean, but it smelled almost pure when she left the shop. She focused on the colors that decorated the box and on the feeling of them in her hand, for if she gave thought to any other sensations in that moment, she would have screamed.

***

Gemma could not paint for days. The desire wasn't in her. She did, however, check each evening when she came home if the box was still on her table. It had not been stolen.

Eventually, she put greens, yellows, and blues on a palette. She made amber, turquoise, and amethyst and brushed them onto a canvas. The image blossomed like spring foliage. While holding a brush, she was able to forget the pains that existed in her like cancer. At night, she dreamt of traveling with her parents to places illuminated by gleaming sunlight or coruscating stars. The worlds trapped within her escaped, and their colors glowed. She made a grassy path that curled between forest and ocean, a field that rippled under the moon, dew drops that glimmered with dawn light, and a man and woman leading a little girl up a flowering hill. Every color was on display except red—that had been blended into the others for oranges and purples, but red did not belong on her creations.

For the first time in years, Gemma felt like she had survived her bullet wound.

She would need money for supplies. There would be no more exchanges at the pawn shop. Gemma took the paintings to a park, showed them to a well-dressed woman who was halted by the images, and begged her to purchase them. The woman touched the colors, not fully believing they were real. Gemma was not certain how much to charge, but she earned enough to buy more canvases.

She brought her next paintings to a coffee shop and asked to display them. The owner agreed, and one worker after another left their station to gawk at the images. They put their reactions into words and told her how the pieces made them feel. Gemma wondered how many people would see what she had created. The answer was few. By lunch, all the paintings had been sold to customers, and Gemma was able to afford a drink of her own.

This carried on until she could no longer squeeze her favorite colors out of their flattened tubes. She needed more paint, but she only had one finished piece, and Gemma knew she had to sell it for all its worth if she hoped to continue. Gemma wrapped the canvas in a towel and took it to a gallery. She implored the elderly owner to exhibit her work and sell it.

That's not how this industry works. How much are you looking to sell it for?

I don't know. Enough to buy what I need to keep painting.

The owner had clearly heard similar stories before. She waited with disinterest for Gemma to reveal the painting so she could turn her down and get on with her day. Gemma shakily undressed the canvas and the forest contained within. A great chasm of disbelief opened on the owner's face. She brought the painting closer, examined the brush strokes on the sunbeams, then held the image at a distance. She looked at it the way Gemma had looked at the forest all those many years ago.

I will give you all the paint you need. Can you make more pieces like this?

***

Gemma was dressed in a short skirt that contorted as she moved about the gallery. She adjusted it when a reporter and cameraman stopped her. The reporter asked about the paintings arrayed on the white wall, all of which had sold. Gemma was unaccustomed to such attention, but she did her best to answer questions. Her name had been omnipresent during the banquet, with many an attendee approaching to gush about her work. Gemma had talked with them between bites of hors d'oeurves—she had known it was rude to gorge herself in such a setting, but she could not recall the last time she had eaten her fill of such incredible food.

What inspires you?

The reporter's question matched that of other attendees. How could Gemma explain the feeling of colors or her connection to places where the earth blushed? What could she say about her past without breaking the revelry of the evening? She gave only a sketched account of her history, then fell silent. Gemma fixed her skirt again and realized she could finally afford a second one. A better one that fit properly. Her cupboard would soon know the weight of canned goods, her refrigerator would soon know a fullness it had long forgotten.

Once all was complete, the gallery owner toasted Gemma with champagne. They spoke of what steps to take next, and then Gemma stepped outside to a city bursting with noise. Traffic flowed like river rapids, headlights zoomed like shooting stars. Artificial colors twinkled on billboards, advertising one product after another. People chatted or stuffed food into their mouths as they walked. Most of them had phones in hand and tapped the glowing screens.

Gemma caught a cab advertising a sports bar with flaming drinks and a hundred televisions. In the back seat, she wondered when she could move to a safer apartment, or if she could shorten her hours at work so she could focus on painting. Gemma pulled out her phone, accepted electronic invites from people she had met that night, then scrolled through posts. She stopped on a pretty picture from another artist, a digital illustration of a nude woman and a mythical beast walking side-by-side in a marble temple. Gemma tapped the screen to leave an artificial heart on the image, then leaned back and drank in the illustrator's work. The cab likewise scrolled down the broadway. Countless signs and billboards flanked the street. Images, often repetitive, often torn or faded, were affixed to brick and stone.

***

Opportunities opened for Gemma, one after another. A gentleman who had failed in his bid for Gemma's work at the auction commissioned her for another piece, which led to another commission, and then another. The director of a stage play hired her to create a backdrop, Gemma's largest work yet. Reviews of the play praised the scenery, claiming it transported the theater audience to a foreign time and place. One of the audience members must have agreed because she hired Gemma to illustrate a book.

Gemma was becoming more than an artist. She was a name, a style, a brand—one not yet paid like those who had played this game for years, but she was thriving. She was invited to conversations, to dinners, to bars. Gemma finally saw herself as a part of the city rather than as an unwanted bit scraped off a plate. She was the wizard of shading and colors, the woman who turned nature into magic. People clamored for her work. Those who could not afford originals bought prints.

How proud her parents would have been if they knew how far she would come. She was living a respectable life like the people who worked in business, in technology, and in law. She ate three meals a day, and her art supplies were never without a color she required. She was finally able to sleep peacefully, finally able to dream.

The fairies in Gemma's phone showed her the extent of her reach. Her work appeared on social media and articles. At first, she was pleased. People far and wide, regardless of wealth, were appreciating her creations. Perhaps she was inspiring little girls and boys to one day create their own magic.

But quickly, Gemma's name became disconnected from her work. People began to attribute the pictures to other artists or themselves. Then came the computer-made imposters. Their colors were bold, but they did not shine. Their trees were tall and broad, but they were not alive. They captured sunlight, but they imprisoned the kaleidoscopic glow rather than radiating it. People adored the imposters, and worse, they falsely claimed they were Gemma's work.

Success left her conflicted. It was as if a dam had burst, releasing her art but also imitations upon the electric world. Art like hers, but not hers, in a million social media feeds. This version of Gemma, her ideas without her thoughts, her name without her identity, moved faster than her. Was this flattery or a curse? If she complained, people chastised her for greed or jealousy. They did not need the stylist to adore the style. This was a difficult lesson for Gemma to accept, that some sought out art as a lover, but most were satisfied with convenient whores.

Then came the businessmen. One wore a crisp, gray suit. He presented Gemma with contracts for her art and promised wealth if she just signed on lines. Gemma saw food in the zeroes and paints in the dollar signs. She was tempted to surrender her creations, but she could not trust the man's spotless clothes, nor the species of his bespectacled eyes, nor the loud, mechanical ticking of his watch. There was no love of art or nature in this man, nor love for Gemma. He only understood money, and she understood what it meant to be used.

I'm sorry. I can't.

You'll regret if you don't.

I'll regret if I do.

His warning left an oily stain. He slithered away to his monetary den, but like all scavengers, he was waiting for the opportune time to feed.

***

Gemma first witnessed the beast while scrolling, scrolling, scrolling through her phone. The machine was a wonder, but it was also a dragon, a wyrm of gears and pistons, a beast of metal and wires. It had plastic scales fastened with bolts and a steel, prehensile neck that arced and twisted. Its narrow eyes shone electric blue. Rather than fire, this dragon—this robot—breathed imitations of art.

The video had been recorded at an art museum in a nearby city. One wing of the building had been cleared out to house this mechanical thing. The dragon writhed over canvases and spat paint, creating multiple images in the time it took Gemma to mix her colors. It vomited entire mountain ranges and oceans. It clawed paths through gardens and sunbeams through forest canopies. When its ruinous creativity was complete, the dragon slumped forward and slept.

A man in a silver vest and silver hat entered the glass lair where the dragon was kept. He chose one of many colorful canvases at the dragon's feet and held it up to shivering applause from an audience. Gemma recognized the painting. It was a changeling of her own work. The trees were too rigid, the clouds oversaturated, the grass too sharp to be welcoming, but the likeness was unmistakable. The dragon had emulated Gemma. A year's quantity of her work lay like welcome mats on the floor.

She felt wrung out like an empty tube of paint.

Gemma bought a ticket for the next available show and traveled to the museum. She waited with the rest of the crowd in a long hall that ended at double wooden doors fit for a castle. On one wall of the waiting area hung a dozen masterpieces from across the centuries, each one progressively newer as they approached the doors. On the other wall hung digital screens promoting the dragonesque robot. The ticket price and dates for the show blazed constantly in the foreground while pictures of the dragon's handiwork fell like raindrops in the background, too swift and too small to be appreciated.

The crowd was abuzz with anticipation. No one seemed to recognize Gemma. One group discussed how well the dragon was able to recreate her aesthetic, but when Gemma faced them, they ignored her, seeing only a stranger. Finally, when the grand doors creaked open, the crowd filed into a broad chamber. The outer walls were tiled with imitations of Gemma's style. Every painting was slightly unique, a minor variation in arrangement and focus, but every line and smear bore her fingerprints. The representation of light and shadows was her signature. The layered colors were her identity.

Most telling of all was that none of the paintings had a single drop of red. As with Gemma's work, strawberries were green and not yet ripe. Apples could be golden or burgundy, but never crimson. Sunsets were never darker than pink. At least a hundred of these parrots hung on the walls, all imitating and mocking her.

The dragon slept in a large, glass box like an animal at the zoo. The crowd formed a circle around the cage, but Gemma continued to trudge from one imposter canvas to the next. The more she looked at them, the more she saw the imperfections. These were leprous clones. Their foliage lacked the subtle blur of the breeze. Waves failed to bend light. Rocks lacked freckling. Sunbeams gave no warmth. The man and woman ...

Gemma froze. There was a painting of a father and mother leading a girl up a flowery hill, but the parents were on the wrong sides. The father was too tall, his hair too unkempt, his attention upward instead of on the girl. The mother stood too upright, as if the little girl swinging from her arm weighed nothing.

This violation, more than any other, bruised Gemma's heart.

Synthetic music blared from speakers. Two familiar men strutted onto a balcony overlooking the dragon's glass cage. One was the man dressed in a silver vest and hat, the designer of the dragon. He waved a champagne glass like a wand as he boasted his creation was the next evolution of fine art. His machine and its computer brain were not held back by the limitations of human artists. It could propagate new masterpieces at an impossible rate, making fine art available to the masses and not just the privileged few. Its speed was its mastery.

The other familiar man on the balcony was the businessman in gray, the one who had threatened Gemma with a contract of his liking. His expression was that of a crowned king surveying his subjects.

The man in silver took suggestions from the crowd for what kinds of natural scenes they wanted to see. He took up a computer tablet and drew spells on its screen. The dragon illuminated its eyes and reared its head, stretching. It counted the canvases arranged on the floor and then pounced upon them one-by-one. It moved in violent throes, belching snow-capped mountains and burnished sunrises. The images were near-sighted changelings of the lands within Gemma's mind.

People pushed past Gemma to lean against the glass and gawk. She, alone at the back of the crowd, wept.

When the dragon was through, the man in silver crossed a bridge to stand atop the glass box. He opened one segment of the cage with a key and climbed inside with the mechanical beast. Dozens of canvases covered in greens, yellows, and blues lay upon the floor. The man showed off one of his creation's changelings, a painting of a pond shaded by trees. The crowd cheered, whether for the image or the accomplishment, Gemma could not tell.

The man in silver adjusted a microphone attached to his collar. He asked a question over the speakers. *Who would like to buy this one*?

The hands of willing bidders rose.

Gemma wailed.

You stole that from me!

Her outburst drew the attention of all who were present. She screamed at the men in silver and gray, accusing them of taking her art for their own gain. She warned the crowd of the mutant flaws of the changelings, how the paintings were illusions rather than magic. The crowd looked upon her as if she were the trickster, the lunatic, the monster. People congregated to the far side of the glass cage, away from her.

The man in silver showed confusion, then amusement. He explained to Gemma she was mistaken. The dragon had a mind of its own. Every painting it generated was unique. It merely learned from artists, just as people had done throughout history, but it was the perfection of artistry.

It does what no human can do. If you understood the technology, you would see how this is a new form of creation, and what's new cannot be a copy.

But you don't understand the art.

The man did not repent. Gemma cursed him and his thievery. She told the people to reject him, but none left the exhibit. Instead, they watched Gemma be apprehended by security guards and forced out of the room.

As she was being shoved, Gemma glared at the businessman on the balcony. The man in gray certainly recognized her.

You had your chance to share in the profits.

***

The museum banned Gemma from returning, but she wanted nothing to do with the dragon's imposters anyway. Unfortunately, the imposters continued to pester her like mosquitos. They would appear and nip her fingertips while she was scrolling on her phone. She saw them advertised in other museums and galleries, and people who recognized the resemblance to her work brought them up in conversation. Worst of all, shops that had once sold prints of Gemma's paintings now sold the dragon's duplicating vomit instead.

The world spoke less of Gemma. She was just another artist, but the dragon was something new and mighty. It broke the constraints of old art. No longer did the splendor of a painting have to be shared. People could have their own unique hills and trees belched upon a canvas. Instead of paying for the invisible ideas of a painter, they could acquire a changeling and still have enough coins left over to afford a good lunch.

Gemma's success did not shatter, but it did crumble. More and more attention went to the dragon. The mutations on its paintings were too small to be seen at a distance. The blues, greens, and yellows were bright enough. The dragon created backdrops for plays, decorations for businesses, and wallpapers for phones. The man in silver was interviewed again and again, and his only genuine creations were the lies he conjured about his inspirations. He could not name the mountains and streams his machine recreated. He did not know the feel of their waters or the scent of their winds. He only knew buyers and the color of their money.

She tried to keep up with the machine. Gemma sacrificed sleep for additional brush strokes, and she toiled to grow her reputation, but she was fighting the dragon's fame without a dragon of her own. Paintings required days to be finished, but excitement for them lasted only a moment. Eventually, her commissions lapsed, and Gemma was once again highly aware of the money in her pocket, the food in her cabinets, and the cost of her rent. She remembered the taste of hunger and the fear of tomorrows. Her newest paintings lost their luster.

In time, even Gemma's original pieces were known by the name of the dragon. Its conquest was complete.

***

The museum's gala was that night, an evening of fine food and drinks. The wealthiest citizens of the city would be there to wag jaws and rub elbows. They would also be bidding on artwork, and the star of the evening was the dragon. Prints of its handiwork were now the decoration of the commoner, but the dragon's fame was great, so its originals demanded a steeper price than Gemma's creations ever had.

Gemma, dressed in soiled black clothes, was a shadow in the alley behind the museum. The front entrance was arrayed in red carpets and dazzling lights, but the darkness allowed Gemma to go unseen. She was once again a vagabond without a home, so she had been haunting this side of the museum, studying its secrets. She had learned the back door's password from workers who stepped outside to smoke, and earlier that day, she had ridden the train with one such worker. There, she had taken the woman's badge from her purse but nothing else.

Limousine carriages arrived at the museum, signaling Gemma's time had come. She leaned from the balcony of the neighboring building and sprayed obsidian-colored paint on the eye of a camera, and then she hurried deeper into the alley. Five presses on a keypad unlocked the door, and Gemma stepped inside the museum's little-known entrance.

She was in the working quarters, a place of bricks rather than art. Gemma heard the clamor of servants preparing the evening's feast. If they caught her, Gemma's plan would be thwarted. She crept past waste bins, then down a hall with sealed boxes of food. Hunger tempted her to take one, but that would make her a common thief. At an open doorway, Gemma stole a peek at the chefs stirring sauces and loading trays into ovens. The aroma scratched the inside of Gemma's empty belly with its claws. The only thing she swallowed was her saliva.

Advancing closer to her goal made Gemma more certain she would be caught, not less. Surely, at any moment, a wandering servant would discover her and raise the alarm.

Intruder!

Guards!

But no shout came. She reached a locked door, this one secured by an electronic box. Gemma opened the satchel fastened around her hips and waved the stolen badge. The door unlocked and welcomed her as a friend. On the other side was yet another hall meant only for the staff. She had to avoid the display rooms of the museum. Security's attention would be focused there, keeping watch while esteemed guests with wine and champagne explored the exhibits.

Two women's voices approached. Gemma ducked into a men's restroom and gave them time to pass. She pushed deeper into the building, thinking of the facility map she had studied. The dragon's den was to the west. She had to keep going.

After another locked door, brick walls and concrete floors gave way to painted drywall and wood. Sculptures and paintings that had been retired from exhibits adorned this area. There were offices and break rooms. Gemma slipped around a corner and faced the back of a security guard. Her heart climbed her throat like a cat chased up a tree. The guard did not turn. Gemma resisted the impulse to retreat and instead tiptoed behind him to another branch in the hall. This was the westward artery of the museum. She was certain of it.

At last, she reached a final door with a sign identifying the dragon's lair. Gemma emerged on the upper floor of a room, surrounded by colors she knew better than anyone. A five-piece orchestra serenaded people in tuxedos and gowns. The man in silver and the businessman in gray were among the crowd, showing off their beast. The dragon thrashed within its box, spewing more replicas of Gemma's art.

There was no time to wait. The guards would quickly be upon her. Gemma hurried along the balcony but discovered the bridge to the cage's entrance was raised. No matter. With a running start, Gemma leapt from the railing. She landed in a loud heap upon the cage, and momentum pushed her toward the edge. The glass squealed as she grabbed for purchase, wearing her fingerprints down to nothing on the slippery surface. Fortunately, she came to a stop, just short of falling into the crowd.

Security! There's a protestor.

Gemma's eyes met those of the men in silver and gray. They were visibly nervous, and that alone meant her foolhardy plan had succeeded.

All the tools she needed were in her satchel. She used wires to pick the cage's lock and threw back the panel. The ladder into the box was not in place, but she was so close. Gemma hung from the opening, swung forward, and threw herself onto the beast's back. It trembled under her and spat paint upon the floor. Gemma clambered up its spine, then its neck. She had to cling with all her limbs to avoid being thrown off. The dragon let out a mechanical, grinding roar, and Gemma shouted over it.

You stole everything from me. You have no idea what I gave to create this art, and you have no appreciation for what went into it. All you care about is taking the money I worked to earn. You're petty thieves.

Security guards were now assembling on the balcony and lowering the bridge into place. They did not matter nearly as much as the slack-jawed guests now watching Gemma, nor as much as the cameras and phones now recording her. She took a brush with worn, fractured bristles out of her satchel. It was one of the oldest she owned, a relic of a past life. She jammed it into one of the dragon's glowing eyes, which caused it to lurch sideways. Her marbled ring caught on a bolt, and she had to struggle to pull her hand free.

Gemma then took out a knife and sliced one of the veins of paint that ran through the dragon's jaw toward its open mouth. Finally, she cut her own wrist and let her blood rain on the changeling canvases below. Crimson splashed on trees, on flowered gardens, on oceans, and on the gray floor.

This is what I gave, and this is what you took.

She cut her wrist again, and then her forearm. Her neck. The flesh of her cheek. The pain was nothing compared to the ache of a trampled heart. If anything, she felt relief at finally stabbing her troubles. Red poured in full display of shrieking guests. Gemma's head lightened, color and light faded from her vision, and then the guards were upon her.

***

She survived her injuries. An ambulance was summoned as well as the police. Gemma was taken to a hospital on a stretcher, then later led out in handcuffs and stitches. She was put on trial and given a fine she could never pay. Gemma worked jobs she detested for the sake of keeping canned food in her cabinets and a roof over her head.

She made art when resources allowed, at least for a while. The man in gray could never take her passion for painting, but it would have been better if he had, for he had taken everything that made painting possible. Now busy with a life she despised, Gemma was a lover with scarcely any time to connect with her love.

As for the dragon, it was repaired. Gemma's fight with the beast was seen on phones around the world, but that brought even greater fame to her foe. Her deeds did have one lasting effect, however. The world became aware of red's absence from her paintings as well as those of the dragon. When the public saw crimson splashed upon the greens, blues, and yellows, they adored it. They begged for it to be added to future pieces, and the man in silver obliged. He changed the dragon's brain, and when it resumed its theft of all Gemma had created, red was boldly present in the images. The crowds cheered and paid even more for the dragon's vomit.

On a humid summer day, Gemma found herself with a rare opportunity to paint. The mountains and beaches were too far away and costly to reach, so instead she sat under a tree in the park. Her canvas was scratched. Her brushes were worn and frail. Her paints were diluted so they would last, which robbed them of their luster. Nonetheless, she was determined to capture the domesticated beauty of the park. The worlds in Gemma's mind needed an escape, lest she go mad.

The scenery took form on the canvas. The colors were wan compared to the vibrant hues within Gemma, but painting was sustenance to her. It was life to her soul. She would put everything she had into the art even if she were alone, but a few children gathered to watch her work.

Gemma tipped the piece toward them so they could enjoy it. One of the children asked if she was trying to make a picture like those created by the dragon.

The question touched her heart like a fired bullet.

Gemma left the park in silence, her painting unfinished. She reached her small apartment before the tears flowed in full. There, she cast her brushes across the gray floor. Gemma curled onto her bed and scrolled through her phone, and her phone wondered if she would be interested in buying changelings from the dragon.

Outside, the city was noisy. Inside, Gemma wept while trying to sleep.

DARK THOUGHTS

The doctor looks down at me with an all-too-familiar expression of sympathy. Not empathy, just sympathy. It takes more than second-hand pain or walking a mile in someone's shoes to feel empathy. You have to trek barefoot across the same hot coals and earn the same blisters to experience that kind of connection. Sympathy is a hell of a lot easier, and it's all I've gotten from civilians, doctors, and counselors since the war. Good for them. People aren't supposed to survive what I went through.

My left hand is wrestling with my right. I clasp them together and force them onto my lap, and that's when I realize my left leg is bouncing. The leg muscles have regained most of their strength, but hell if I know whether feeling will fully return. It's like living with permanent anesthesia in that limb, except all I get is a recurring limp rather than relief. The pain still knows where to find me, especially when the weather's cold.

The doc squeezes the bridge of his nose. His receding hairline provides a lot of real estate for the wrinkles on his forehead.

"I'm sorry, Mr. Bayer. I'm not sure what else I can try to ease your nightmares. The treatment helps patients nine times out of ten, but ... well, some people are unfortunately stuck holding the bill of being the odd man out."

There it is. I yawn, which brings out tears. When I wipe those away, I feel the gym bags under my eyes. "It is what it is, Doc. I told you the first time we talked I wasn't gonna get my hopes up. I've gotten enough bad news and sorries to know to expect them. Nothing I can do but soldier on."

I rise to my feet and offer a handshake. It's a formality rather than a show of respect and thankfulness. If I were to give in to my impulses, I'd be cussing him instead. I'm tired of wasting my time on doomed treatments from people who don't understand what it's like to be hunted and tortured by your own injured brain. I've come to accept my scars, my aching joints, and the tingling nerves in my left leg, but I'd kill for the chance to sleep peacefully like I used to. Every night is a roll of the die for nightmares, and the die has less than six sides.

"Hold on, there's someone else who might be of service to you." Doc opens a folder and hands me a printout. It's a lot of text divided into boxes. The fuchsia company logo at the top reads *brAIn-wave Tech*. "Give these folks a call. I'll put in a referral. This treatment option is brand new and unconventional, but if they select you, the service is free."

"Free? In other words, they're looking for guinea pigs."

Doc shrugs. At least it's an honest response. "Hard to say. New treatments come with risks, but from the studies I've read, this technology could be to trauma what penicillin was to infections."

"The trauma is whatever. I just want the nightmares to stop."

Doc pats my shoulder, just below the burn scars. "Those things are connected. You've got to beat one to cure the other."

I'm about to hand the printout back to Doc ... but for some reason I keep it instead. Psychologists and physicians have been tossing me back-and-forth like a hot potato for years. I know I shouldn't get my hopes up, but it feels like my cure can only come from outside the box. Hopefully the company's technology is better than their advertising—that brain logo at the top of the page looks like it got beat with purple ugly sticks.

Doc clicks his pen and scrawls his signature on a document. The *scritch-scratch* of the sharp, metal pen tip sends an excruciating surge down my spine. I involuntarily search the room for fiery eyes, and my heart rate hits the accelerator. Once the appointment is over, I hurry through the lobby so I can get to fresh air and shake off the tension. I don't say goodbye to the secretary on my way out, not that I could. My teeth are chattering hard enough to drive nails through my fillings.

***

I make the phone call to *brAIn-wave Tech*. This leads to multiple interviews where I confess my physical, psychological, and family history. My answers must prove I'm sufficiently screwed-up because I soon receive confirmation I've been selected to test their developmental implant. The procedure is better than free ... it'll earn me a thousand bucks. If nothing else, I'll have booze money.

On my in-person evaluation date, I arrive at a modernized building with brick ribs, tall windows, and two added wings. The lobby is cavernous, and my footsteps echo when I approach the front desk. The bare walls glow with nature scenes shot out of projectors. The lady at the security desk is cheerful but efficient. She has me take a computer survey with so many questions, it makes college entrance exams seem quaint by comparison. She then leads me to an examination area, where I'm met not by doctors but by three nerds dressed in black lab coats and holding tablets. The room is less a medical office and more a corporate computer server. Lights glow and blink behind mesh and glass doors. The air conditioner struggles to keep up with the thermal oven coming from god-only-knows how many computers. An octopus of wires hangs from the ceiling, and below that is a massage bed illuminated by a dazzling, rainbow glow. When I sit on the bed, I can barely see the dark, shadowed walls because I'm half-blinded by a ring of LEDs and monitors pointed in my direction.

The three technicians all seem to be in their twenties. Two are males, one Indian, the other a white dude in glasses, and neither could be mistaken for anything but engineers. The female technician, on the other hand, is an absolute scoop of sugar. I give her a smile, but I'm not much of a looker at the moment. They had instructed me to get my head shaved before the appointment. My scalp hasn't been this naked since basic.

The brunette technician nods toward the encompassing ring of electronics and then waits for my response. When I say nothing, she asks, "What's your initial impression, Mr. Bayer?"

"It's a bit much. I'm sure you understand what all this does, but to me it's a circle-jerk of technology."

She cringes. "That's ... one way of putting it. I thought you were an electrician."

"I am, but I'm not much of a computer guy. It's different."

"Fair enough. Well, I'll let you know this represents only a fraction of the computing power we'll be relying on. There are processors throughout the facility that will be assisting in the data collection and interpretation. We'll essentially be reading your mind in real-time."

If their computers are reading my mind now, they'll realize I don't care about the pitch-and-spiel, just the results.

They ask me to remove my shirt. That would have bothered me during earlier treatments, but I've stopped caring about the scars. The worst one is the burn, which looks like someone took a cheese grater to my left shoulder and worked their way to my sternum and spine. Like everyone else who sees the marks for the first time, the technicians pinch their lips and hide their initial reactions. They actively lock eyes with me and avoid mentioning the lizard skin.

Brunette places a band of sensors around my neck. They remind me of rosary beads. She then glues the metal sensors to my chest. A line on one of the monitors transforms into the peaks and valleys of a heartbeat. She avoids the scars as much as possible and tugs a couple sensors to test the hold. "Are you doing okay?"

"I'm fine."

"You're surprisingly calm."

"What am I supposed to be scared of? We're not cutting yet."

"Let me know if I can do anything to make you more comfortable."

I keep my initial response to myself, but I can hear the guys from my unit whispering *rollcha*—short for "roll for charisma." It was our good-luck chant whenever one of us broke the ice with a girl. "You could take me to dinner after this is done. That'll make me comfortable."

She gives a lukewarm smirk. "I don't think my boyfriend would approve."

I read something else in her then, an impression that she was the type who protested the war during college. My life would be less hell if she'd won that fight, but my experience with pacifists since returning home is they talk big about supporting troops while mostly just using them as political ammunition. They say they don't blame the soldiers for the blood that was shed, but when they speak long enough, especially after a few drinks, the truth works its way out of the BS.

The technicians lay me back and then fit a strange cap over my head. It looks like a hair net decorated with glass beads. They pull the octopus cables down from the ceiling and connect them to the hair net. Monitors come to life with toggling numbers and fluttering lines. A map of my brain emerges.

"This is very brave of you," Brunette says. "Your assistance has the potential to help millions."

"Brave? Anything for my country, right?"

"Actually, for the whole world, but also for you individually."

"Our evaluation will involve a sleep study," says Glasses, the white guy. "If sleep proves difficult, we can provide a sedative."

"I got shut-eye in muddy trenches and in the backs of trucks. I'll manage. The problem I have now is staying asleep."

Glasses gives an unimpressed, disinterested nod. I'm probably not going to be the biggest fan of this guy. Glasses says, in a tone like plain, lukewarm oatmeal, "For this evaluation, you'll need to recall the source of your trauma so we can register the effects. Using that data, we'll train your implant to counteract the harmful mental responses. I apologize in advance if the process triggers negative stimuli, but it's a necessary step toward achieving results."

"I've been recycling this purgatory for years. What's one more day?"

The technicians finish their setup, then take seats at the boundary of the outer shadows. Their fingers dance on their tablets. The Indian technician reaches up and points to the monitor showing a blue-and-yellow map of my head. "Here is your brain."

"Yeah, that's the bastard responsible for my problems."

The technician pauses. "You can watch the physical responses on this screen while you talk."

Glasses says, "One second ... Okay, Mr. Bayer, please state your name."

"Specialist Alyx Bayer."

"Excellent, the microphones are picking you up. If you're ready, please recite the story. Explain the incident that led to your recurring nightmares."

The peaks on my heartrate monitor are already sharpening. My hands clench and release like artificial hearts. I realize within seconds there's something worse than the dumbstruck bedside manner of a psychologist or doctor unsure what to do next—there's the cold scalpel stare coming from Glasses. As I talk, I feel less and less like a veteran telling my story and more like an animal raised for research.

"I was in the 41st Infantry Division, Seventh Army. My deployment was four ... no, almost five years ago. Went through some engagements and firefights, lost some friends. It was war, and it's as awful as everyone says, but it's different living through it than watching it on the news. I saw stuff that'll stick with me ... you don't need to hear about all that."

"We do," Glasses says. He types on his tablet. "It's relevant to your case."

It feels wrong to unwrap the stories, like I'm breaking protocol or about to turn these civilians into collateral mental damage. I choose one piece of the past, enough to scare them off from probing further. “I don’t think the early parts are relevant, like this one time that rockets came down on our position. My unit took shelter and did alright, but the blasts hit a house. We checked for survivors, and ... like, I’m sorry, there’s no good way to put this. We found a family and their dog smeared on a wall. It was that kind of stuff.”

Sparkles of red filter through the blue-and-yellow brain map. The technicians all take notice of the color change. I’m itching for a cigarette. “Can I smoke in here?”

“No,” Glasses says. “It’s against company policy, and it’s bad for the equipment.”

“Damn. Anyway, that stuff bothered me, but that wasn’t what gave me the nightmares. Our orders had us guarding a village on the flank of the main contact line. It was a mining area out in the country, lots of poverty, you know the deal. The enemy would occasionally ball-up and take shots at us with mortars or artillery, and we’d respond. The worst fu—excuse me, the worst darned part were the drones. We got a taste of what the Russians went through in Ukraine. It was always a race to jam and evade them. They sounded like swarms of wasps, and if they managed to sting you, you go home in a bag or one limb lighter. The bangs were bad enough, but you grow numb to that. The anticipation for the swarms became the worst part, you know?”

The peaks on the heartrate monitor zipper closer together, and my heart is taking a crowbar to the inside of my ribs. The brightness of the monitors strengthens, making the shadows behind them thicken. I brace for what comes next, when my memories wake.

“Are you okay, Mr. Bayer?” Brunette asks.

I tug at the sensors on my chest. “They’re getting tighter.”

"We haven't adjusted them, Mr. Bayer. Do you need to pause for a moment and gather yourself?" She offers a tray with crackers and a small cup of water. "Snacks and drinks are available to you if they'll help."

"Or," says Glasses, "for what it's worth, pressing on now is ideal for studying your body's physiological effects."

I roll a cigarette that isn't there between my fingers. "One morning, the enemy goes for broke. There's a mining tunnel we don't know about, and they manage to get a group into the trees outside the village. They don't lead with artillery or drones because they know the sound will give us time to take cover. No, they put RPGs into the industrial supplies, probably thinking it's our ammo."

My jaw is cramping. I squint because the monitors are flaring too bright. The room's closing in on me, and the urge to escape rakes claws under my skin, combing through muscle fibers. The ghost pains are resurrecting and blurring my vision. That's when I notice red indicator lights on each of the six cables connected to my head ... they're staring at me. "It's here," I mutter through short, pent-up breaths.

"What's here?" somebody asks.

I shouldn't have mentioned that. "Nothing ... That first blast hit a methanol tank. I don't know if you're familiar with that stuff, but when it burns, the fire's invisible. Kippy and Diego were closest to the ambush. The guys avoided the blast, but when they ran for cover, they suddenly dropped to the ground and started rolling and screaming."

It's hard to think over the buzz of the computers, which is starting to remind me of the drone swarms. I try to ignore the screams because I know they're just echoes. My fingernails involuntarily dig into the padding on the table, and the mortar rounds of my heartbeat are sending shockwaves all the way to my skull. It feels like somebody's talking to me, but I'm focused on getting through what I need to do. There's no stopping the momentum now.

"Our boys tried to rescue them, but the enemy opened up with small arms fire, keeping us at bay while those guys burned. It was surreal. No flames, just them screaming and heat waves making the forest look like it was rippling. Artillery came in then, further pinning us in place, making us stationary targets for the insane swarm of drones, but ... the ... the guys are cooking alive. I need to save 'em. I'm in the back of an armored truck, nothing heavy, just something we use for recon and transport. I lay suppressive fire on the trees. Calder's the driver. He backs us toward Kippy and Diego, trying to put our vehicle between them and the enemy. A round comes in, and I have just enough time to duck into the belly of the truck before the blast tackles us sideways. The boom's deafening. For a split second, the front windshield is bright white, and it backlights Calder when his head bursts like some kind of gory water balloon. That's when I get knocked cold."

Even though I'm holding my eyes shut, the six red glows are getting through my eyelids and searing my retinas. I smell charred flesh. It's here, the thing that uses my nightmares like a lair. It climbs on top of me, pinning me to the examination table with its leathery mass. My chest is getting crushed. I have to sip oxygen mid-sentence as I talk faster and faster.

"When I come to and regain hearing, there's a constant slur of drones, bullets, and screams, but not from Kippy and Diego. They're not moving anymore except for the wavering heat, and their skin's charred black. I can't move either. The truck's upside down, and the armor that got punched inward by the blast crumpled onto my back and legs. The sharp part of the metal is squeezing me like a bug in tweezers. I smell blood and feel oil leaking onto me. That's when the enemy finally rushes out in force and overwhelms our position plus the little village. I hear 'em using guns to delete anything that moves, so I play possum where I'm at. They find me, and they think I'm a goner, but just to be sure, they light the spilled fuel. That's when I get the burns."

I catch my breath and then describe the weeks I spent trapped inside the wreckage. Over several days, birds and dogs cleaned burnt flesh off Kippy's and Diego's bones. In the truck, I was endlessly threatened by the tip-tap of claws from rats and crows waiting for me to succumb, and I had to fight off the bravest scavengers so they wouldn't make a meal of my trapped legs.

No help showed up. I'd been abandoned as warzone debris. I was constantly hungry because most of the provisions in the vehicle got destroyed, so I had to ration what little food was within reach. When water ran out, the tacky saliva in my mouth became so thick it almost suffocated me. The skin on my groin blistered and peeled because of constant contact with urine-soaked fabric, and I could feel shit moldering in my underwear. If I moved too much, the metal would slice into my leg, and if I had tried to force my way out, it would have stripped the flesh off my thigh like I was peeling an orange.

For weeks, I baked during the day and froze by night. I not only knew I was dying, I felt it through my whole body, like a soda going flat. My only hope was to atrophy fast enough to escape before thirst finished me. I should have ended up with the same fate as the other guys in my unit, but Death got bored of all the easy kills from the war and decided to take its time with me.

The only reason I outlived the torture was because the Army retook the village and eventually found what was left of me.

The rescue didn't bring much relief. For a long time, the treatments at the hospital barely touched the pain. Rehab was brutal. Whenever nurses turned down the lights, my vision got boxed in by this imaginary metal frame like I was back in the vehicle, watching my friend roll and scream. The images set like cement in my head.

I finish the story, which leaves me exhausted and sucking wind. I've shared what I went through, but I can't possibly explain how intensely it's causing me to reexperience the pain. As I reawaken to my surroundings—I lurch from the table, shouting because the shadows are looming over me, watching me with six eyes. Gravity slams me to the floor. "Oh, god, I thought you were ... phew. Sorry."

"You thought we were who, Mr. Bayer?" It's Brunette. The six eyes belong to the technicians, who had crept up on me during the flashback, close enough to touch me. As they help me to my feet, Brunette says, "We tried to get your attention, but you were gone to us. Are you hurt? Do we need a nurse?"

I shake my head and slump against the table. The Indian technician brings me water, which I down entirely. Glasses talks on-and-on about how my sensors had lit up like Times Square and provided plenty of data, but I'm too beat and shaken to care at the moment.

Brunette is studying me. "During your recollection, you said something about '*it's here*?' Can you please explain?"

"Did I? I don't remember it."

"You did. There was a moment during the story when you said, 'It's here,' and you sounded mortified. What was that about?"

I chew up a few seconds, and then make my confession. "It's some boogeyman that stuck with me because of the experience. The locals called it the Uyanka. They warned us to avoid the forests at night so it couldn't get us. They were more afraid of that thing than of us with all our firepower. It took a lot of asking to convince someone to explain the Uyanka. It's a spirit of death that's made of darkness and shaped like a mantis. It has fiery eyes that lure you in if you're lost, and that's when it attacks. Listen, I know it's probably some superstitious BS, but I swear when I was trapped, I saw the damned thing watching me from the trees. There was something out there making this clicking, giggling noise like nothing I've ever heard, and at night it would come close and scratch the wreckage like it was trying to get to me. I'm not keen on mentioning that part because it makes me sound crazy, but even if it was fake, it still became a real part of my nightmares. I carried that monster home with me."

***

"That stuff's the death of our brains," Parker complains over my shoulder. He's an old Navy seaman who's a regular at our VFW. "People use what's easy instead of thinking for themselves, and where's that get them in the long run?"

I reply with a solo-digit salute. Parker gets the message and goes back to massaging his beer and yelling at the Dodgers on TV. He doesn't like that I'm using the *Write-Boost* feature on my phone while dictating an email. It's an AI app that rewrites my semi-coherent drivel as a message with better phrasing and focus, making me sound about forty IQ points smarter. It was originally promoted to wounded warriors and others whose injuries and disabilities make typing difficult, but pretty much everyone my age uses it, at least for official correspondence. We all avoid it on social media, though. No one wants to sound like an idiot in school or business, but no one wants to sound like a robot to their friends either.

If Parker thinks dictation improvement is a ridiculous use of AI, what would his opinion be of the technological witchcraft implanted in my brain? My hair has regrown long enough that I no longer wear a hat to hide the surgical scars. Per contract, I'm required to provide weekly status reports to *brAIn-wave Tech* so they can monitor my health and make software adjustments. I don't need Parker listening in to that conversation, so I leave the bar counter for the privacy of an empty corner booth, out of his earshot. There, I finish the email.

"The first few months improved things a lot ... or, umm, seemed like a big improvement from what I used to experience. Umm, the nightmares only happened maybe once every, like, ten days or so, but lately it's regressed so the nightmares are one or two times a week. My impression is kinda split so far. This was the first cure that made a real difference, and thanks for that, but I'm worried it's just a temporary reprieve that'll keep trending back to where I used to be. Can you do more of that calibration crap or no?"

The computer transmits a more intelligent version of my request. I doubt the report will come as a surprise considering my implant perpetually uploads data to the company. The information they collect is proprietary ... part of my deal with the devil. Hopefully they're looking past embarrassing dreams and focusing on addressing the harmful ones. Before the war, I never would have participated in this kind of research, but I have nothing to lose. I'm tired of my brain fighting a self-destructive guerrilla war against itself. Initially, the implant seemed like the cure, or at least a good-enough solution. I was finally getting decent rest between the bad bouts, but that progress has been slipping away.

I still don't get good vibes from *brAIn-wave Tech*, but I have no choice besides relying on them. They're the last horse I can hitch my wagon to.

***

Back in my one-bedroom apartment, I pop open a beer, drop into a recliner, and turn on the end of the Dodgers game. The umpire calls strike three on a low pitch, and Parker is undoubtedly cursing at the VFW's TV. Fans like him hate the idea of bots taking over the umpire's job, but their outrage over bad calls is why I'm certain it's only a matter of time before the switch is made.

A light breeze sneaks in through the window, which I always keep slightly ajar. Shutting and locking it would cause me to hyperventilate. The bedroom light is on. I never turn it off. Darkness makes it too easy to get caught in a deep, violent sleep.

My head starts to hum and vibrate. It's subtle, gentler than an electric toothbrush, and it means my implant is downloading an update. The sensation is followed by three chimes, an indicator of an incoming message. My brain's electronic passenger can transmit audio to my inner ear, which means the voice in my head is more than a figure of speech. I receive a slightly robotic message.

"Good evening, Mr. Bayer. Thank you for your communications and continued assistance. We apologize if our latest self-learning iterations have not provided satisfactory support. We remind you this is a work in progress, and full

recovery is likely to require many months. Be assured, with each day, the technology grows smarter. We are performing a comprehensive update at this time, one which should expedite your progression. Please continue your routine check-ins, as these will optimize the rate at which we can meet your needs. From all of us at brAIn-wave Tech, *congratulations on being a part of the future. The mind is the key to human potential, trademarked.*"

I take a drink from the beer can. "Hey, brain-thingy. If you can inject audio into my ears, does that mean you can also hear when I speak?"

The buzzing finishes. No more replies.

By the end of the baseball game, my bladder demands attention. The route to the bathroom is through the bedroom, and out of habit, I check my angles before entering ... the bedroom is where the enemy likes to ambush me. The bed's a mess. A lot of guys I served with start their days by perfectly making their beds, but I'd rather enjoy the luxury of a crumpled blanket. The drill sergeant doesn't get to live rent-free in my thoughts forever—a new inhabitant occupies that space now.

I keep the bedroom bare, with little tying me down to my present location. On one side of the bed is a lampstand with a broken pull-chain. On the other side sits a tall, oak dresser with random items on top of it ... my gummies, candles, a framed photograph of my parents, an alarm clock, my Purple Heart medal, etcetera. The middle drawer is where I store a pistol as well as my t-shirts. A footlocker and a computer desk fill out the rest of the room. There's a single window, and the Venetian blinds always have at least a slight opening so I can peek at the outside world.

After relieving myself and flushing the toilet, I reverse course toward the bedroom. That's when another vibration tickles the inside of my head. It must be another software update, but this one's stronger. It feels like static in my teeth fillings. My scalp ripples, and my eardrums pop and sizzle. I listen for a new message. Instead, the bedroom light flickers, then goes dark with a loud bang. Glass shards tinkle on the floor. Did the lightbulb burst, or was that incoming fire? I drop prone and crawl to the threshold.

The rocket-fuel rush of adrenaline is abusively familiar. I'm back on the battlefield, being sawed in half by my fight-or-flight responses. My body is rigid and thrumming like termite-infested lumber. I'm sweating, and the bathroom floor is ice cold against my belly. I crawl partially into the bedroom's darkness, intent on collecting my weapon from the dresser even though I'm questioning my actions. What exactly am I supposed to shoot, my sense of dread? I'm alone in this apartment—

Ahhh! *Ahhhh*!

The darkness screams. The voice is sharp but muffled. It hits an octave that can only be achieved by dying, suffering people.

Ahhhh! *Help*! *No*! *No*! *Help*!

I recognize that voice. It's been festering inside me for years. Kippy's rolling and thrashing in the dirt like a squeezed maggot, trying to put out the invisible flames. Burns and shrapnel wounds are racing each other for the chance to claim his soul. He's close enough that I witness every detail of his death, but he's too far for me to do anything about it. There's nothing physically paralyzing me this time, but my legs associate movement with agony. It's like I'm caught in metal teeth all over again. If I try to slide out, my skin will be stripped off like soaked jeans.

Using only my arms, I drag myself toward Kippy's voice. He can't possibly be here, but I must check anyway. I can't fail him again. Every object in the darkness is a vague shape wavering behind curtains of heat. I hear the shadows. They're breathing ... crunching ... cackling. I smell the gross, industrial tang of gasoline fires being doused by blood puddles. The red numbers from the alarm clock reflect off glass fragments beneath the lampstand ... six of them. The red specks blink in unison, and then they blur as my eyes involuntarily twitch side-to-side.

Kippy's voice quiets. It's replaced by the buzz of drone rotors ... or maybe insect wings. Pointed, dagger feet scramble across the ceiling, sounding like chisels on metal. It's the same inexplicable pitter-patter that taunted me night after night while I was trapped over there, waiting to die.

I'm face-down when something impossibly strong and tall grabs my head. It lifts me like I'm nothing more than a doll, and then it squeezes, driving needles deep into my nerves. I try to fend it off but swat only air. My skull is at the brink of shattering. Terror spasms cascade through my body and shake my limbs. I'm suspended in or by nothing. As soon as I scream, shadowy mandibles are forced into my open jaw. They bite through the roof of my mouth. There's a flashbang migraine, and then a sound like slop being stirred as the thing eats through the center of my brain. The mandibles explore. They reach bone and break through like a hammer through ceramic, then crumple the pieces. Razored tongues noisily slither and scoop out the insides of my skull, everything except the implant. Finally, mercifully, I lose consciousness while being overwhelmed with indescribable, violating pain and sounds.

***

I wake and raise my head. I'm on the floor of my apartment, sprawled in the doorway between bedroom and bathroom. Sunlight slices through gaps in the blinds. I run my tongue over the roof of my mouth, which is intact. When I roll over to a seated position, I come to the damp, muddy realization I've soiled myself. My body feels like it went ten rounds with a boxer.

There's dried blood on my right palm and fingers. I touch glass slivers sticking out of the skin. Larger shards are spread around the lampstand, and the light is off ... I hadn't imagined that part. The rest of the experience had been a visceral nightmare, too real and agonizing to be called just a bad dream. I've been rebaptized into all the horrifying sensations I endured overseas and in the military hospital. Kippy's cries are gone but fresh as ever in my thoughts.

I sob and catch salty, burning tears in my hand. They wash blood off the embedded fragments of glass.

***

The phone plays several minutes of chippy, synthetic waiting music before a male voice answers. It's Glasses, the technician from *brAIn-wave Tech.* "Good morning, Mr. Bayer, how may I be of assistance? I understand you called with a concern?"

"Concern?" I laugh coldly. "Hoo, that's putting it lightly. No, I called to ask what the hell you guys put in my head? I've dealt with flashbacks and nightmares for a while now, but they have nothing on what happened last night. It was so bad, I passed out on the floor."

"Did you go to the hospital?" he asks.

"No. I cleaned myself up, including the damn mess in my pants, and then I called to speak to you."

"Okay, good. Given the early state of the research, it's advised you work exclusively with us to address any health problems."

"So you can hide any screw-ups?" I ask.

The technician is quick in his answer. "No. Medical practitioners outside of *brAIn-wave* are unfamiliar with the tech and how it interacts with the human body. I'll remind you, one stipulation of your contract is that you're obligated to come to us for non-routine medical care. Legally, you're not permitted to disclose our research to anyone outside our company."

I squeeze my phone like it's that nerd's neck. "I called because of a serious issue, and your first response is to threaten me with lawyers?"

"It's not a threat, Mr. Bayer." He's as cool as pennies in a freezer. My raised voice fails to budge him. "I'm simply stating procedural requirements you agreed to. Following them is in the best interest of both yourself and the company. It will protect the integrity of the research."

I sit back and rest on the edge of my counter. A bang in the street below my apartment causes me to eye the window. "So that's how this experiment's going to be? I call when there's a real problem, and your only concern is the research, not me?"

"Calling is an option, but email would be more efficient."

"That's not the point, you—"

"Mr. Bayer, listen to me. This is crucial. You have metal components and electronics linked to your brain. If a doctor who doesn't understand that treats you, it could be catastrophic. For example, if he were to put you through an MRI, the machine would rip the components out, taking half of your skull with it, or at the minimum, it would cause interference and short-circuit your brain."

I exhale slowly. It does nothing to calm me. "I *said* I didn't visit any doctors."

"Good, but it was important I affirm that point first. Now, please explain what occurred."

I describe everything from the previous night, both the stuff that happened and the stuff I imagined. I make certain to stress the experience was unlike any previous nightmare. I couldn't escape by waking up. The dream was so real, it seemed like it could genuinely kill me. The flashbacks hijacked my senses. I smelled gunpowder, Calder's rotting corpse, and the interior of the wreckage. I felt the flames and the blood dribbling from my wounds. I tasted acid from an empty stomach eating itself.

Glasses asks questions with more curiosity than concern. I pace my living room as I answer them, and several times I shrug under my clothes, which feel confining. At some point, I run my fingers through my hair and touch the scar from the implant.

"Mr. Bayer, are you still there?"

I must have drifted off. "Yeah, I'm here."

"Here's what I suggest. Continue tracking your symptoms and reporting them via email. Notify us of concerning developments."

"So, nothing different. No changes. Thanks a friggin' bunch."

"Listen. My guess is the AI took your last report into account and calculated that now is the optimal time to increase the aggressiveness of your treatments."

"Can you dial it down?"

"Not precisely. The program makes informed, executive decisions through a combination of exterior inputs and internal, developing logic. It's like a person in that you can't force it to make a choice, but it can be convinced with enough strong arguments. Your negative experience from last night is already being accounted for by the implant, but it's also weighing that against a composite of decades of psychoanalytical research. Right now, it's as if you're being individually supported by all the best therapists in the world, and we don't always know what's best compared to that kind of expertise."

"But you're the one in charge and paying the bills. Tell your little digital therapists to lighten up."

"That may not be beneficial to your recovery. I ran a query on your treatments, and there are suggestions of EMDR modalities, which necessitate a patient revisit their trauma through guided recollection."

"I'm familiar," I say. "I tried it. I tried everything."

"Not with any technological advantages, you didn't. Our system has determined you would benefit from a more confrontational treatment."

I halt in my pacing. "So, you acknowledge the implant is to blame for last night."

Glasses doesn't skip a beat. "No, your trauma is to blame, but recalling it highlights vulnerabilities that your implant can then fix. Think of it like white cells going after a virus. The body will exhibit symptoms due to the conflict, but in the end, the host is cured. You're on your way to normalcy, Mr. Bayer."

"Last night was too much. Please, there's gotta be a better way to lower the intensity. I don't care if it means the process takes a little bit longer."

"Hmph. Fine, I'll forward your suggestion, but remember *you* came to us because you couldn't figure out how to get past this. I would think someone in your position would be ready to defer to an expert, especially one trained on thousands of pages of human research data. Trust the implant, Mr. Bayer. It will get better. There's light at the end of the tunnel. I must be going, though. Please continue to let us know if you have any concerns or questions, but email is the optimal way to reach us. Thank you."

The click hits like a thrown rock. I'm left with a silent phone and the feeling I've been discarded like a candy wrapper. I fear how many more intense nights wait between me and the supposed "light at the end of the tunnel."

***

During lunch break, I sit in my truck at a local park, eating the sandwich I packed before work. The weather is pleasantly warm for autumn, so I roll down the window to let in the breeze. A bunch of kids are squealing like excited primates at the nearby playground, and adults are jogging with their dogs or riding bikes. This should be a delightful pause, but then I see *it*, and my skin wriggles.

The mantis is hanging in a face-down, hunting posture on the trunk of a tree. I'd missed it while it was stationary, but now its nibbling the needles on its arm, cleaning them like a serial killer prepping her knives. It reminds me of the bugs the guys in my unit used to mess with during boring shifts as perimeter guards. We called them Little Uyankas, insect Grim Reapers. Back then, it was easy to mock the creature as superstition.

The mantises were basically pets. Guys would feed them worms we dug up from our trenches, and Calder once stuffed a captured mantis into the pants of a rookie named Stirling. The kid woke up, dropped trousers, and hopped around the trench to shake it off. I laughed so hard, I sprained a rib.

Now, here in this park, I'm tempted to use my concealed pistol on the vicious, little creature. Unintimidated, it tilts its head to face me down.

A grasshopper thrums past my widow and descends to the worst possible landing spot, a fern directly beneath the mantis ... no one ever accused grasshoppers of being smart. It stares upward dumbly like a tourist in a big city. The mantis tenses and checks the surroundings are clear. The last thing it looks at before creeping down the tree is me, like it wants me to watch what's about to happen. Once within striking range, the mantis pauses ... and then explodes onto its prey.

The grasshopper is not without its own dangerous mandibles, so the mantis chews sideways through the other bug's mouth first. The bites move like an eraser through exoskeleton, and then through an eye. When the mantis reaches the brain cavity, the grasshopper finally stops kicking and trying to spread its wings. Slowly, the prey vanishes into the garbage disposal mouth of the predator.

Cold, steel memories tighten around my ribs. I involuntarily reposition my legs and shake my chest and arms. My tongue contracts, and I taste metal saliva at the sides of my mouth, a pregame swig of coming vomit. My scars stretch and threaten to reopen. After dabbing sweat from my brow, I drop my half-eaten sandwich onto the passenger seat and activate my truck's ignition.

***

Dinner is a six-pack of Coors and two cigarettes. It dulls my worries, but when I lie down, it also turns my mattress into a pool float. I ride the internal waves until they calm, and then I wriggle awkwardly to the dresser side of the bed.

Earlier that day, I bought a second lamp for the bedroom, just in case the other one decides to burn out another bulb. I plug it in and recline under the dual spotlights. The additional illumination has the added benefit of making the cracks in the ceiling less noticeable.

The night's chilly, but as usual, I rely on my sweatshirt and sweatpants for warmth. I don't mind using sheets, but the heavy comforter stays bundled at the foot of the bed. Rest never comes quickly, even when I'm so tired it feels like I've got elephant tranquilizer in my system. I roll side-to-side and rearrange myself in different poses, guessing at the right combination for sleep. My neighbor yells about something. His outburst reminds me of another one that occurred at my apartment building—that one turned into a shooting incident. That incident messed me up for days. I want to ignore the neighbor, but soon, all I can think about is whether my gun is where I left it. Is it loaded? Is the safety on? One more roll toward the dresser can't hurt, right?

I jostle the drawer open and confirm my firearm is still there, still ready should I need it.

Eventually, my mind wears itself out enough that I dip into sleep. Years of awful dreams have trained me to never go into a deep rest. I cling just beneath consciousness in case flashbacks return, so even in sleep, I'm aware of my surroundings and the passing time.

That's why, when both lamps begin flickering in the middle of the night, I come to immediately. The flashing turns the ceiling cracks over my bed into long, black bolts of lightning. It's likely a wiring issue. I don't want to fix it now, but there won't be any sleep with those pulses burning like acid through my eyelids. Grumbling, I start to tighten one of the bulbs but immediately release it. The plastic is way too hot, especially for an LED.

On top of that disturbance, the neighbor's yelling again. If I have to walk to his door to make him stop, he's not going to enjoy the encounter. Instead, I slap the wall and hope he gets the signal. "Quiet down!"

Initially, it seems to work, but then the jerk responds with a delayed high-five slap on his side of the wall. It doesn't stop with one hit. He lands another slap, then two, then three and four. The impacts morph into smaller, crisper, repeated sounds. He must be using his fingernails instead of a single palm to strike the wall. The noise resembles hail on a window ... or talons as crows hop on a wrecked truck, waiting for the trapped passenger inside to become easy pickings. The tapping climbs to the top of the wall, then spreads out and skitters across my roof ... how could the neighbor get up there, unless ...

The thing needling across the ceiling on tiptoes suddenly drops with a thud big enough for a rhinoceros. Paint chips ricochet off my forehead, and dust rains like confetti ... or like ashes from a house burning with your buddies inside. The thing above me belly-flops over and over. My neighbors aren't reacting to the commotion, so maybe I'm the only one who can hear it, but I could swear it's real. With each vibration, the lamps flicker and my eyes quake. My heart fires like an artillery barrage, and I taste fumes and death when I gulp air. Violent memories are returning. I can't move. If it's a dream, I'm not waking. All I can do is grab fistfuls of the bedsheet and accept what comes next. This is the part where I get forced to relive the past.

The claws hurry to the area above my bed, and wiry feelers probe through the ceiling cracks. They widen the thin fractures into rifts. That's the moment when both lamps burst and go dark, leaving me with a dim view of the hateful creature emerging from above.

My senses recall the battlefield. The sounds of humming drones and cawing crows. The stench of rodents fighting over Calder, pulling rotten meat out of his bloated corpse. The sight of two birds standing on Diego's slack-jawed face. One pries out his eyeball and holds it in its beak like a lollipop. The other bird beats its wings and pecks the bloody, spindly fibers attaching the eye to the socket.

The sensory flashbacks are memories, albeit ones with sharp teeth, but the demonic thing being birthed through the cracks is different. I never saw it like this during the war, but its hostile presence was a constant in the forests beyond our forward operating position. It was why we always assumed the enemy was close. It was also why we didn't joke about Uyanka superstitions when things got quiet at night.

Logic says there's no huge, dark monster digging through my ceiling, but my trembling body thinks logic should shut the hell up.

The other side of the opening is on fire. Six red eyes stare out of the inferno, and four pitch-black legs sprout from the ceiling. The legs move like liquid shadows down the corners of the room until the creature is standing over me. Next comes thick, spiny claws. Those scoop up my head and cradle me for a moment, and then they clamp my skull, driving spikes through bone. I want to scream in agony, but the shadow quickly thrusts its mandibles into my mouth. It tears my cheeks so my jaw can be forced unnaturally wide, and it bites through the roof of my mouth so it can get to my brain. I feel and hear it slurping blood and cranial fluids. Tongues swim like electric eels in the fishbowl of my skull. Pain sizzles in every cell of my body. Fighting the shadow is hopeless. I can't wriggle out from under its immense mass, and the pressure of it on my stomach makes me want to vomit.

***

The first phone ring is a shock paddle bringing me back to life.

The second ring forces me to sit up. I'm in bed, in my apartment. The room is dim, but the window blinds are glowing with sunlight. I hurt everywhere, especially my head and my right hand, which is again bloodied. Plastic slivers from the busted LED bulbs are sticking out of the skin. Am I the one breaking them in my nightmare stupors? My shirt is soaked with sweat, and my boxers and bedsheets are soaked with worse.

The third and fourth rings pull me out of bed. I find my cellphone tossed in the corner with its charge cord still attached. The clock on the screen reads 10:34 AM. The date indicates I only slept one night, but it seems longer. The caller is my boss. I'm four hours late to the construction site, where I'm supposed to be installing new wiring.

"Bayer, where the hell are you?" He's angry, but he also sounds relieved I picked up.

"Sorry. I screwed the pooch." My scars are sizzling. I move my phone to a hand that isn't throbbing from plastic splinters "I had a rough bout last night."

"Like what? Drinking? A bad date?"

"No. Flashbacks. Nasty ones. I couldn't tell what day it was when you called, let alone what time."

My boss is a fellow veteran. He doesn't deal with the same issues as me, but he's understanding. There's a pause, and then, "Just get here as soon as you can. People are depending on you."

I nod to myself. "Got it."

The call disconnects, and I sink into a sigh. After removing lightbulb shrapnel with tweezers, I hop into the shower. The warm water loosens my mind as well as my muscles. Last night is a mystery. It's impossible to separate what was imagination from reality. I think back to what Glasses said about the implant eliminating my trauma like it's an infection. The six fiery eyes that stared through the ceiling cracks were the same eyes that watched me suffer while I was trapped.

Did I bring the Uyanka home with me in my mind? Did the implant release it?

That's impossible, right?

***

The last two weeks have been torture. Since the implant's latest software update, I've had five nights of tangible, realistic nightmares that end in me being devoured by a shadowy mantis. Each time, the misery lifts me just short of waking up, dissects my brain, and knocks me unconscious.

The polite, professional messages I've sent to *brAIn-wave* have gotten me nothing but hollow email promises that the implant is solving my trauma. That's why I turned off *Write-Boost* in my last status report. I wanted every four-letter word in my response, butchered grammar and all. I let them know I'm coming to their office, and I won't be leaving until they fix the damned thing they put in me.

I slam my truck into park at the company's visitor lot, right beside several black government vehicles. Even though I'm ten minutes early, Glasses is outside to greet me. He looks pissed, but that means we finally have something in common. A bit more problematic are the armed security guards flanking him on either side. Off to my right, four police officers step out of their patrol cars and keep watch.

Glasses gives his villain speech as I march up the sidewalk. “Mr. Bayer, it’s a pleasure to see you, but not necessarily under these circumstances. We here at *brAIn-wave Tech* are dedicated to healing mental illnesses that affects millions around the world, but we cannot complete that work under threat. We have counselors inside who would be happy to assist you through your current ordeal.”

I’m done being offloaded to new counselors. I start to point a finger at Glasses, but that might look too hostile to his security detail. “I didn’t threaten you or anybody else.”

“Your email correspondence, which has been saved to our records, indicates otherwise. We realize our research means engaging with individuals who are not of sound mind, but surely you understand we must take precautions when a patient warns he will ‘hunt down’ the people in charge.”

The security guards step forward before I can completely close the distance to Glasses. “Bad choice of wording on my part, but it’s just an expression. I’m not going to shoot anyone, obviously.”

“People say that, and yet gun violence persists.” Glasses is standing rather casually and out in the open for someone supposedly afraid of getting shot. “Let’s see, you also stated you were going to be a nightmare to us in return, and you were going to rip out your implant and shove it somewhere. I cannot expose my team to that kind of harassment.”

I swear the guard on Glasses’s left cracked a brief smile. He looks like the kind of guy who would agree with my position if we chatted over a beer. “C’mon, that’s obviously a joke.”

"Mr. Bayer, you're not allowed to enter our facility without an invitation. That alone makes this serious."

"No, here's what's dead serious." I jab my temple several times. "*This* is horrific. I want it out. I can't take it anymore. The nightmares are as bad as the original incident. It feels like I'm dying all over again."

"That's the purging process I warned you about. It's an unfortunate necessity. The insight of hundreds of experts has determined this is the best course of action for your healing—"

"Shut up about the goddamned experts already."

"That would mean taking the side of ignorance."

I lunge at Glasses, but the guards are quick to shove me in the direction of my truck. "What if it's not the experts that screwed up but you, huh? How am I supposed to know you're not doing this intentionally to me for secret studies? It wouldn't be the first time a company lied to patients. Or to veterans."

That's the first comment to get a rise out of Glasses. "We've been nothing but honest with you, Mr. Bayer. Displacing frustrations with your situation onto us is counter-productive. I'm sorry, but eventual peace of mind is going to require some discomfort."

I shake the guards off me. "Up yours, all of you. Where do you get off telling me it's just some discomfort like it's nothing. You haven't gone through a fraction of what I've been through. You have no idea what real pain is. Take the implant out. I'm done with this. I was better off wasting my life with shrinks."

"Your mental training regimen is incomplete. If we remove the implant now, you risk being permanently stuck in this state, nightmares and all. The only way out of this tunnel is to keep going forward."

I've failed. I argue for several minutes, but it's wasted

breath. Eventually, the police officers and security guards team up to physically encourage me to vacate the property. Glasses watches me go, which means he watches as I kick several of their company's shrubberies on my way to the truck. When I peel out of the parking lot, I leave rubber and smoke behind. The tire marks are a final plea for help or a warning, their choice. I'm angry enough to do something stupid, but I'm also terrified. The Uyanka is waiting for me at home. Somehow, I know it's never going to let me reach the light at the end of the tunnel. I don't have what it takes to escape it twice.

***

"Bayer, help! Bay-yer. Bay-yer."

Kippy's voice rouses me and raises my head. My vision vibrates momentarily. I had crashed on the living room couch in hopes that sleeping in a new location would weaken the nightmares. Now the nightmares are calling me to their lair in the bedroom.

"Bayer, help!"

I say, "Kippy, you're dead," but I also put my feet to the floor. "You've got to let me go. You're not real."

The bedroom's sudden silence is an equally strong plea for help. I lean back and want to shut my eyes, but they won't close. I try to recline, but my body slides to the front of the cushions as I do. I'm a human wrestling match between two needs, one to save the ghosts of my men, and the other to avoid the pain at all costs.

"Bay-yer."

The Uyanka's in the next room, ready to ambush me.

The inside of my skull buzzes like dragonfly wings, and then it goes still. I await a message. Instead, I hear a distant scream from Diego. "*Ahhh! Agghhh! Put it out!*"

Kippy is groaning.

Calder whispers, "*They need us.*" His voice is so close to my ear that I lurch off the couch and turn to face him. He dissipates as soon as we lock eyes. A claw scratches the back of my neck, turning me again to nothing.

"I can't, I can't, I can't." I'm muttering and begging. I sound pathetic. "I can't, I can't, I can't ... damn it, no more."

If *brAIn-wave Tech* won't keep up their end of agreement, then neither will I. I'm going to the hospital. MRIs are out of the question, but maybe a doctor can give me drugs to get through the next nightmare. Hell, I'll call the news and be a whistleblower for what's going on. I need my phone. It's charging on the counter. I wake it up so I can search for the news station's email address, but the screen stays black. It's *on* and glowing, but it's black, and holding the power button causes ... I drop the phone and let it crash to the floor. I swear I just saw tiny, reddened glimpses of Kippy's, Diego's, and Calder's faces, each in duplicate. Six crimson faces in total, and all blinked in unison.

"*Bayer, help.*" All three are crying. "*Bay-yer.*"

"Please, stop," I manage to say with a tightening throat. "Guys, I can't anymore."

Black lines sweep along the wall and stomp on the couch I had been lying on. A thicker shadow, bristling with spikes, scratches the kitchen cabinets. I shuffle toward the exit, but the shadows dart to cut off my path. It's herding me ... the Uyanka, the dream, the implant, whatever it is.

Static skitters like insect legs on the inside of my ear drums. The light fixture that illuminates the living room and kitchen belches smoke ... smoke that smells like human flesh and clothes cooking in a gasoline fire ... until the bulbs detonate, sending me sprawling to the floor.

The pitch-black shadow legs step closer.

The nightmare can have my apartment. I make a break for the window. If this isn't a dream, I can yell for help, and if it is a dream, I can ... well, that option won't hurt in a dream. I beat the shadows to the window, but it's a hopeless plan. Hundreds of black crows are fluttering outside, all with red, burning eyes. One crow lands on the windowsill and shows me its prize. A long strand of veins and nerves hangs from its beak, with a human eyeball at the end, swinging like a clock pendulum.

The pistons in my heart are hammering. Shadows are shrinking the room, so I hurry to the bedroom. I know it's a trap, but I have no choice, I can't let them touch me. Once inside, I slam the door and lock it. I need to barricade myself in and hold out. I shove the footlocker against the door, but it's too light. There's got to be another way to escape, one I haven't thought of yet, and if I haven't thought of it, neither has the thing in my head.

What about the neighbor who had been yelling? If I heard him, he can hear me, right? I sprint to the wall and hammer it with my fist. "Help! Help! Call the landlord. Get someone in my apartment, quick."

No answer, at least not from the neighbor. The responding bang comes from the bedroom door. The shadows on the other side are battering it. The door booms and rattles on its hinges. The footlocker budges. I need something heavier ... something heavier ...

The dresser! I've been leaning against it while pounding the wall. I claw my fingers behind it and pull. It shudders one inch toward the door. The next pull is on the right side, which slides a few inches. Another pull, and the left side lurches half a foot. I just need to keep working it side-to-side, steadily rotating it across—

The dresser grunts to a halt. It won't budge. One of the floorboards is sticking up and blocking it. I drop to my knees and coax the dresser's leg over the obstacle, and just then, I spy a bristling shape in the void under my bed. It's Uyanka's other claw. It lashes out while I'm barely holding up one corner of the dresser. I can't dodge it. The claw scrapes my burn scars, making the flesh remember the inferno. Teeth gritting, I fall against the bottom of the dresser. Its bulk keels forward. The drawers all eject as far as they can, spilling their contents. The stuff on top of the dresser crashes around me, and then the dresser collapses onto my back. The oak landslide presses me facedown against the floor, and just like that, I'm back at the start of all my nightmares, trapped beneath a weight.

I can't convince my lower body to move. It's not paralysis. If it were, I wouldn't be feeling the bruises spreading through my legs and back. The dresser's heavy, but not as heavy as metal. The reason my muscles won't respond is because they're too familiar with this trap. Attempting to move means agony. Are there water bottles and MREs within reach?

The room darkens, not because the lights go out but because the Uyanka stands over me. Its eyes are heated needles in the back of my head. Claws delicately cut lines into my flesh. The Uyanka is patient ... but I'm furious and desperate.

"No! Not again!"

My arms are free, just like in the wreckage. I feel around for anything I can use as a tool to give me leverage—and I make the mistake of glancing under the bed. Kippy, Diego, and Calder are lying there in the darkness, smoldering. Birds and rodents have eaten away parts of their burned cheeks, giving them mangled, exaggerated smiles. They're staring at me with black, empty eye sockets, and the only thing moving on their bodies is their lips.

"*Bay-yer*," they chant together. "*Bay-yer, help us.*"

Shadows squeeze my head. Needles skewer my eyelids and force them open. It wants me to see them. I'm grabbing everything in reach. Socks. Shirts. The frame with a picture of my family. Cold steel ...

It's my pistol. Before the Uyanka can stop me, I turn off the safety and bring the gun's barrel to my chin. My pulse is thundering at Richter scale levels. I'm panting, shooting spittle with each breath. Is this a dream or not? Will I wake up? I yell, and I stretch that yell into a long roar as I put pressure on the trigger.

And then I release the trigger.

I'm still panting, but I manage to say, "Not today. You don't get what you want. Maybe tomorrow if I'm still here, but not today, you asshole."

I slide the gun under my head like a pillow. It'll be there if I need it. No point in shooting the Uyanka, I've tried that before.

What else can I use? My Purple Heart medal is a blur at the edge of my vision. It gives me another plan, one I'm barely aware of because my brain's being flooded with agonizing memories. I part my regrown hair, put the edge of the medal to my surgical scar, and begin sawing, sawing, sawing. It's a numbing sensation, but skin eventually gives way. My forehead warms. Liquid red spreads across the floor, but I keep sawing. I'll peel bone and rip the implant out if necessary, so long as it means I regain control of my thoughts.

The Uyanka isn't stopping me. If anything, it seems all-too-pleased to watch me do this, so I stop. The blood's still running, and maybe that'll be my ticket out of here, but that doesn't help me get revenge on the implant. What else is within reach? There's the base of the lamp, which is plugged into the wall. Electricity, maybe?

The shadows loosen their grip on my head. The Uyanka takes one step back.

The answer was so obvious, I should have realized it sooner. I am an electrician, after all. What's the worst thing for an electronic device buried inside me?

I unplug the lamp and accept the resulting darkness. I then twist and force the Purple Heart medal into the socket until violent cramps seize my arm, my chest, and my head. My teeth clench as I arch and spasm. A mental lightning storm blinds me to my memories ...

***

I wake up on a strange bed. Is this a medical office? I have an IV in my arm, but I'm encircled by a ring of computers and monitors. Three people in black lab coats are staring down at me as if they were waiting for this moment. One of them is a rather cute brunette. She's holding a weird device that resembles a voltmeter. The second person is Indian, and the person at my feet has thick glasses.

"He's coming to," the brunette says.

The guy in glasses nods. "Mr. Bayer, can you hear us?"

"Who?" I ask.

"Specialist Alyx Bayer. That's you."

"That's me?" I ask. Why does that sound wrong? What's my name? Is that really it? Did he identify me with a military rank?

"Do you know how you got here?" the guy in glasses asks.

“No. Where am I?” I try to move but can’t. My wrists, ankles, and chest are strapped to the bed. That’s not the worst part. My memory is hollow. The more details about myself I fail to recall, the more panicked I become. What were my parents’ names. What’s my address? Am I married? I’m hitting blank walls.

“How were you originally injured,” the guy in glasses asks.

“I don’t kno—what are you doing to me?”

“It’s nothing *we’ve* done, Mr. Bayer. You did this, and we saved you. For your own safety, the implant decided the proper course of action was to perform a memory wipe. On the plus side, your nightmares might be over. Unfortunately for us, the wipe corrupted our research.”

The restraints are becoming increasingly worrisome. “What implant? What nightmares?”

The guy in glasses holds up a wire probe. For some reason, he reminds me of a mad scientist flicking the cylinder of an injection needle. “You’ll understand in due time.”

MOTION DETECTED

Makenna ran her fingers through her daughter's wooly hair, gently so as not to wake Angeline. The spirals were impossibly soft, as light as vapor. She reached deeper into the curls to stroke Angeline's scalp but touched more clouds. *Strange.* Makenna rose to one elbow and woke to gravel reality—she was alone in Angeline's bed, hugging pillows and blankets that barely clung to her daughter's fading scent.

Not so many years ago, she had been rising with morning sickness. What she would have given to return to those days, which had seemed horrible at the time. Now her mornings were a daily ritual of grief twisting and squeezing her innards. Peace was nocturnal, but hell woke at dawn like a rooster and screamed.

She spilled tears onto Angeline's pillow, and not for the first time. As a child, Makenna had been a notorious sleepwalker, and that issue had returned in adulthood since ... *since.* She often woke in Angeline's room, breathing dander more precious than gold.

Seven years with her had not been enough.

She managed, yet again, to get to her feet. After grabbing a robe from her own room, she trekked down the cold hall with a thousand pounds of heartache sitting on her diaphragm, crushing her stomach. The hall was too long, and the stairs were too tall. There were too many rooms in this miserable house. Too many walls from which to hear echoes of herself and nothing more. It was supposed to be a vessel filled with laughter from a family of four, maybe five.

Makenna slammed the pantry shut after grabbing ground coffee. What was the point in being quiet? There was no one else to wake.

This home had been a dream once, nestled in rolling hills with farm fields and piebald patches of forest. Neighbors' houses were scattered at a distance, close enough to know you weren't isolated, but far enough for privacy. Makenna had loved having room to breathe without a coven of nosy, old suburban ladies judging her actions, decorations, or music. Her husband, Zion, had claimed to adore the change as well. He could be a programmer from anywhere with an internet connection, so why be tied to his old cubicle in Albany.

That same internet connection had been used to find a new career in Georgia and a new woman, perhaps not in that order.

After Zion left, he practically amputated all communications. Makenna liked to think it was shame that caused him to barely call Angeline, but she couldn't be sure. Zion had made only two trips to visit their daughter, and during the second one, she had been sleeping in a casket. When he came face-to-face with Makenna at the service, his eyes had done the talking. They asked, "How dare you fail our daughter like this? You're supposed to be her mother, her protector. Her death is your fault, you murderer."

Makenna had responded to the silent accusations by giving Zion an audible slap. She would have struck again if family members hadn't pried them apart.

The coffee machine gurgled and spat caffeine oil. Makenna gathered milk, sugar, and a spoon. She was a shark, she had to keep moving through this purgatory to breathe. After preparing her drink, she stood in the center of the kitchen, warming her hands on the mug, staring out the window. The pond across the road was almost perfectly round and sat below an amphitheater of beech and ash trees. Cotton candy fog drifted across black mirror water, not unlike the steam atop Makenna's mug. Mr. Bankman, her kind, elderly neighbor, had given Angeline permission to play on his land, stating he missed the old days when his kids were young and did the same. Angeline had loved that pond, but too much. That was where she had drowned. Now it was a memorial. If it were on her property, Makenna would have filled it with cement and chiseled Angeline's name at the center.

She carried her coffee to the porch, set it on the railing, and stared down the beast that was the pond. While sipping her morning drink, she scrolled through photos on her phone, happy memories now rendered into prickling regrets. One of her favorites showed Angeline swinging from a tree without a care in the world. After wiping her eyes, Makenna shared the image to her socials along with a message, *"I'll never stop loving you, baby. Wish I could leave this world and be with you now."* Replies were turned off on her accounts. She had never felt lonelier, and yet she had never been less interested in hearing the opinions of others. It seemed like those who had never lost anything worse than a pet were the ones with all the advice. People had said so much to her since the funeral—it was their turn to listen and just let her be.

When back in the kitchen, Makenna slid her phone to the center of the table, opened her laptop, and cut into the jungle undergrowth that was her email inbox. Messages got deleted, others were organized by the accounts she managed. She had just reached her stride when the phone vibrated and lit up with a notice. It was probably a text from her mother, addressing the post about Angeline. Makenna sighed into her coffee mug and drank the cold remainder of the brew. There wasn't time for emotional discourse. Makenna's boss had given her space to grow numb and adjust to this new life, but patience only held back unemployment for so long. The only thing worse than living alone in the house would be losing it.

But it wasn't a text from her mother. The phone read *Motion Detected.* The security camera on the front doorbell had picked up movement. Neighbors wouldn't be visiting at such an early hour, so Makenna figured it was probably the local deer out for a morning stroll ... except the doorbell suddenly filled the empty home. *Tiiing-tonnng.*

Makenna cinched her robe tight and tiptoed to the door. There was no peep hole—one of the reasons she had insisted on having the security camera installed in the first place—but she put her faith in the chain lock and opened the door an inch or two.

"Hello?"

Silence answered. No "Good morning," or, "It's me." Just a bird clearing its throat somewhere in the distance.

"Hello?" Makenna repeated before pushing a curtain aside and checking the porch through the window. The only thing that seemed to be waiting for her was the fog, which shifted in place like an impatient trick-or-treater. Makenna threw open the door and stuck her head outside, only for a few seconds. The fog dispersed, thinning the veils between her and the pond across the road.

Had she been ding-dong-ditched? Makenna returned to her phone and touched the *Motion Detected* alert. It brought up the doorbell camera's view of the porch from a minute before. There weren't any obvious figures in sight, but there was a dark blur in the mist. It could have been an animal that jumped past the sensor, or a person that ran to the far end of the porch with their hair trailing. Makenna studied the image as she moved around the house, checking every window for a glimpse of the culprit. All she found was more mystery.

***

Makenna's heart was racing. As she doubled over and drank air, she touched her jugular vein and felt the highway traffic of her pulse. Sweat dripped from her curls, ran down her back, and soaked her bra.

It felt both good and terrible to be exercising again after years of lethargy. She'd finished her two-mile jog while dusk set fire to the hills. Makenna caught her breath on the stone path that connected the mailbox to her porch. She eyed the front entrance. Not for the first time, she thought back to the dark blur captured in a still image. She had tried to watch a replay of the video, but the file was corrupted or inaccessible, further cementing the mystery.

As she climbed the porch steps, her phone, which was strapped to her upper arm, buzzed. Makenna knew it was another *Motion Detected* alert, a combination of the camera spotting her and the phone being within range of the Wi-Fi signal.

The door had an electronic keypad just above the traditional deadbolt lock. Makenna was about to punch in the combination—Angeline's birthday in reverse—when she got a premonition to check the door. The handle turned unopposed, and the door drifted open. She was so distracted by everything wrong in her life, she had forgotten to lock the door before leaving.

It wasn't until she was fully in her living room, headed toward the shower, that Makenna had another thought—what if she hadn't forgotten to lock it.

"Is anyone here?" she asked involuntarily. She could have kicked herself. If someone had broken in, the last thing she should do is make them aware of her presence. Her phone buzzed then with a new message, making matters worse. Makenna grabbed her umbrella from its holder to use as a weapon. This was Zion's fault—he had left her alone to fend for herself.

Makenna crept room-to-room, wielding the umbrella like a samurai sword. One of the kitchen cabinet doors was ajar. Had she done that, or had a thief looked for expensive plates and glasses? Her laptop was awake—had someone tried to log in? One of the picture frames on the living room wall was tilted. A shoe seemed out of place from where she had left it. The smart display on her refrigerator was shuffling through family photos, a feature she had turned off because the pictures were a fireworks display of painful memories. Her gun was upstairs. If she called the police, they probably wouldn't arrive for another twenty minutes or more, and she wasn't even sure someone had broken in. It was more of an intuition ...

Her phone buzzed again. She pulled it from her armband. Five *Motion Detected* messages demanded attention, so when she felt sufficiently certain the house was clear, she selected the first one ... an image of Makenna on the stone pathway, hands on her knees after the jog. The pond and forested hillside filled the background. Makenna wasn't alone in the photo. Behind her, hovering above the road, was a dark, wispy smudge, one like the anomaly that had dashed across the camera's eye a few nights prior. It bore the suggestion of a person, like a figure's dissolving shadow, but it gave the impression it was watching Makenna.

She scrolled to the next image. Makenna's arm filled the right side of the frame. She was entering the house. The smudge couldn't be something on the camera lens because it was in a different location, closer, larger. Now it was hovering near the mailbox, and suggestions of limbs and a face marked the dark mist.

In the third image, the anomaly was on the pathway. The contrails at the bottom were denser and seemingly touching the stones, walking. The face was more distinct, recognizably human but not truly recognizable. The upper whisps darkened and curled. A vague hand clutched the chest as if the shadows were a coat to be closed against the cold.

Makenna hurried to the living room to look outside for herself.

In the fourth image, the anomaly was closer and sharper still. It was as if someone had dropped black watercolor paint onto the view and etched the details of a person into the mess. The figure was both part of the shadow and within it. Its size and distance were difficult to judge because the darkness did not give off shadows of its own.

In the fifth image, the figure was climbing the steps to the porch. None of the details were quite right, all smudged, stretched, blurred, and partially erased, but its humanness could not be doubted. Eyes—not quite oval, not quite balanced, not quite anchored in the face—gazed at Makenna through the camera's lens. The hand was reaching forward and pointing toward the bell.

Makenna was just about to turn the doorknob when—

Tiiing. Tonnng.

That sound, paired with the reaching figure on the phone, was a bath of ice water. The chime was followed by a croaking nose, like someone trying to force out words but forgetting how.

Makenna shuffled left, leaned over the small, decorative table at the entrance, and pulled back the edge of the curtain. Using the narrowest, subtlest of peeks so as not to draw attention, she tried to catch the person ringing the doorbell.

No one was there. The porch was barren.

Makenna recoiled, more confused than disturbed. Her brain fumbled the puzzle pieces it had just been handed—no, not puzzle pieces ... jagged, glass shards from a stained-glass window whose picture was too shattered to be deciphered. When she heard *knock-knock-knock*, she opened the door on impulse. A gust of wind entered, but nothing else. The figure staring up from Makenna's phone was absent from the actual porch.

She exhaled in a hypothermic stutter and slammed the door, causing a framed photograph of Angeline to drop from the wall. On impact, the frame spilled its glass guts. Makenna carried the broken treasure to the second floor where, with gun and phone at hand, she checked the perimeter in every direction for strangers ... or anomalies. The gorgeous fields and woods that had lured her into this trap seemed empty. The pond that had taken her daughter stared back. She was surrounded by beauty with teeth, isolated from the world by a wall of open acres.

The rest of the day was a slow release of tension. Normalcy returned. That night, she opened a bottle of wine, hoping it would drain her mind and help her sleep. When she swirled the glass, she noted the drink was just as dark as the shadow that had rung the bell.

***

"Mama," Angeline whispered.

Makenna woke, not in her bed, nor in Angeline's room, but standing like a mannequin on the living room rug ... the same rug Angeline used to lie on while creating stories with her stuffed animals. Makenna had been interrupted while sleepwalking. It was still nighttime according to the darkness outside. Her legs burned with fatigue. How long had she been holding that position? She felt violated by her own sleep, used without consent to wander the world.

"Mama."

There was the whisper again, but this time it wasn't a dream, right? She was already awake. How had she heard her daughter? Makenna wanted to run and scoop her up, to rub her face in Angeline's hair until her cheeks were sanded down to nothing, but she reminded herself that was impossible. Angeline had been gone for months. The police had located her body in the half-submerged bushes of the swollen pond. They had dragged her to the shore and breathed into her discolored lips. Paramedics had used electric paddles and made her small, frail body arch off the ground.

The voice had to be a lingering effect of the dream, and yet when Makenna turned, she half-expected to find she was not so alone after all. Perhaps she wasn't. There, on the hardwood floor, was a faint trail of damp footprints. They had followed, or walked beside, Makenna in her sleep. The final two prints waited directly to her left, shrinking as they dried to nothing. She brought her arm around the empty space at her hip. The hairs on her forearm stood upright, and a chill nuzzled into her.

"Mama."

Angeline's whisper touched Makenna's ear like ice on a fever. Her aching legs unlocked. She limped toward the kitchen and braced herself against the sideboard. Where had the voice come from? Makenna didn't want this to be just a dream. It had been too long since she had heard that precious voice, and she replied to it. "Angeline?"

"Mama." From the door? "Mama, look what I can do." No, it was coming from the kitchen, specifically the table, where her laptop sat open. There were other signs of recent activity, like a knife lying across a peanut-butter-and-jelly sandwich under construction. Those hadn't been there when Makenna went to bed. One slice had a mix of strawberry and grape jam—just the way Angeline liked it. The silverware drawer was open, as was one of the refrigerator doors. Only now did Makenna realize the appliance was beeping, begging her to shut it and salvage whatever cold was left. Condiment bottles had been knocked onto the tiled floor, and also a carton of milk, which was bleeding white through a crushed corner. A dishtowel had been dropped into the sink. Cups were set in a row on the counter, half of them upside-down.

"Mama, I can jump so far." Angeline's giggles bubbled from the laptop's speakers. The room plunged twenty degrees as

Makenna rounded the table and saw what was on the screen. It was security footage from the doorbell camera. Angeline was running and leaping off the porch. She picked herself up and hurried to the steps to do it again. The footage was from earlier that year.

Angeline wasn't the only thing moving on the screen. Large files were being uploaded to a folder. They were named *YouShouldSeeThis_0100*, *YouShouldSeeThis_0105*, and so on, over a hundred of them, and the status bar was only half finished.

She should see what? Was she being hacked or attacked with ransomware? Makenna wanted to immediately purge the files like rotten produce from the fridge, or like cobwebs in the shed behind the house. But she also wanted to know what she was dealing with. Makenna selected one of the uploads. It had a video file extension.

"What the—"

The question congealed before she could finish it. The latest uploads were from a date she couldn't forget if she tried, the twenty-third of May, the day Angeline drowned. The numbers writhed like intestinal worms in her gut. Her fingers rusted an inch above the keyboard. What cruel trick was this? Makenna hit delete for the file she had selected, then deleted another, but the contents of the folder were swelling like an infected wound. She hit cancel on the upload, but files kept coming. One got selected without her input, and it expanded to fill the entire computer screen.

It was another video clip from the doorbell camera. The initial view was of the back of Makenna's green sweatshirt, but that quickly shrank as she leapt from the porch and bolted down the stone pathway. The sun was not yet above the horizon, but dawn light colored the road ... and the trees ... and the pond, which slept unstirred by a breeze. The water's surface was as flawless as a cut diamond until a police officer jumped into the water and waded toward submerged branches. His movements fractured the stillness, sending seismic waves across the liquid mirror.

Watching the video, Makenna felt her throat tighten. The Makenna in the recording screamed at the pitch of utter despair.

She exited the video and deleted the entire folder with genocidal hatred toward its contents, then shrunk into the deepest recess of a chair. Her head toppled to the table, and there she dissolved into a waterfall of tears. The occurrences of recent days were no longer simply strange. Someone was trying to get under her skin. The pain was all-consuming, just like it had been after Angeline's passing.

"Mama, I'm here."

Angeline's voice lifted Makenna by her chin. It had come from the front entrance this time.

Tiiing. Tonnng.

Her tormentor was outside, in the middle of the night.

Fear was the only emotion capable of budging her from her grief. Rather than going to the door, she scrambled upstairs and ripped her phone off the bedside table. The charge cord pulled free with it, whipping her shin. Makenna skipped the *Motion Detected* warning and went straight to the live camera feed. She took in a breath, ready to shout at whoever was on the other side of the screen ... but she swallowed that breath.

The shadow had returned to the porch, its features clearer than ever, all fringes trimmed down to a human shape. It was Angeline, staring through the camera and into the hole in Makenna's soul.

"I'm here, Mama. Don't worry about me."

The temperature of Makenna's tears changed. She fumbled with the phone, nearly dropping it. She found the *Talk* button. "Baby, baby, it's Mama. I'm here."

She was on her feet, headed to the stairs.

"I'm cold, Mama."

She needed to hug her daughter and kiss her. That was her only thought. "I'm coming, baby. I'll let you inside."

"You can't, Mama."

"Of course, I will. I'm gonna warm you up, and you'll be fine."

She jumped the last five steps and hit the floor like a sledgehammer.

"No, because I drowned."

Those words twisted the blade that had been buried in Makenna for months. She ran for the door but slipped on one of the wet footprints. Her balance gave out. Makenna crashed shin-first into the leg of the couch. Blunt pain rushed through her bones all the way to her chest. The phone escaped her and skittered across the floor.

Makenna grabbed her lower leg, groaned through clenched teeth, and crawled toward the phone. The shadow on the camera was moving side-to-side.

"Hold on, baby. I'm coming."

"You deleted me, Mama. Don't do that."

The files. That had been Angeline's doing? "I'm sorry. I didn't understand."

"Daddy deleted me too. He didn't want you to see me go."

Zion?

"Bye, Mama." The shadow turned and skipped down the stone path, in precisely the same way Angeline had done a hundred times while alive.

"Don't go!" Makenna pleaded. "Angeline, wait!"

But the shadow kept skipping deeper into the darkness, fading. By the time Makenna got to the door, Angeline was nowhere to be seen. Makenna limped across the road and onto the neighbor's property. She struggled through mud and tall, stiff grass to the part of the pond where Angeline used to catch frogs and salamanders ... where the police found her inside the cage of a water bush. The memories were vivid ... Angeline with her butterfly net and bright smile, scooping animals out of the water and muck. Angeline on a hot day, cooling her legs despite the slimy tickle of pondweed. Angeline ... dying in the water because Mama had foolishly checked the wrong parts of the pond and moved on to the woods too quickly.

She wouldn't make the same mistake twice. Makenna searched every inch of the shore and shined her phone's light into overgrown vegetation. When she waded into the water, it soothed her now-bruised leg but stung where the swelling flesh was bleeding. The only eyes that glowed in the flashlight beam were those of creatures who used to swim to escape her daughter. Shivering, Makenna refused to give up until dawn once again confirmed Angeline was gone.

But she wasn't crazy. The recordings from the security camera proved Angeline had been there.

The house was punishingly quiet when Makenna returned. Rather than going upstairs to her room to shower and change out of wet, muddy clothes, she inspected the damage to her shin. It wasn't broken, but the injury was going to plague her for weeks. She needed to get the swelling down. Makenna went to the refrigerator, and just before she reached the ice machine, it grunted to life, causing her to jump. Ice chunks cascaded off the drainage grille and onto the floor, and a picture of Angeline appeared on the touch display.

"Angeline?" Makenna asked, hoping.

Ice slid across the floor. Angeline spoke no more.

***

Makenna was reclined on a beanbag chair in Angeline's room, halfway between sitting and lying on her side. She rubbed the ears on Angeline's stuffed cheetah. These days, the room's grayish-blue walls reminded her of rain instead of stone. Everything was tidier than it had been in real life.

She considered the number on her phone and had been doing so for over an hour. Makenna finally welled up the resolve to press *Call*. The phone dialed twice, enough time for Makenna to rethink her decision a dozen times.

Zion picked up on the other end. He was at work or someplace public. People talked in the background. "Hello? Makenna?" His voice, once warm and husky, was now chilly and gritty. When she didn't answer right away, he asked, "Can you hear me?"

"Yes, sorry." *Is he really the right person to speak to*? "Zion, I need to ask you something."

"I didn't do anything," he said. "I didn't touch your bank account or nothing, just like I promised."

"It's not that. It's about the night Angeline passed." *Passed.* That was the heaviest synonym she could manage.

Zion forced out a loud, hissing breath. "You don't really want to get into this, do you?"

"It's important."

"What if *I* don't want to get into it? Talk to a counselor or something. I'm aching too."

Now it was her turn to breathe. She held it for a moment, let the pneumatic pressure propel her forward. "It's not that." She rolled to her other hip. The beanbag chair crinkled under the shift. "After it happened, you looked at the security footage and deleted it—"

"What are you accusing me of?" His question cut her off like a swung axe.

"Nothing, nothing." Was it nothing? Why was he being defensive? "I just want to know what you were thinking when you deleted the videos."

"I was thinking how sick they made me." She could hear him switching the phone to a different hand and ear. "It was horrible, and I thought me ... and especially you ... didn't need to see that ever again. It was bad enough I had to go over it with the cops. Listen, the police watched the footage, too, and took a copy. I didn't do nothing."

"I didn't say you did."

"Then what's this phone call?"

Makenna squeezed the cheetah's ear. "I don't know. You're sure there wasn't anything you were keeping from me?"

"Nothing. It was an accident, that was all. You *have* to let this go. Look, I'm sorry how things went at the funeral, okay?"

They waited for each other to make the next move. This was how every conversation played out now, dancing around the jagged pieces of their shattered romance.

"I gotta go," Zion said.

"Yeah, me too."

"Talk to someone if you need to, but I don't think I'm the right person to help, got it?"

"Yeah."

The phone clicked. Makenna set it down, hugged the cheetah to the underside of her chin, and let the walls rain around her.

***

Tiiing-tonnng.

This time, Makenna was expecting the bell. She opened the door to a balding white man with a gray moustache. His buttoned shirt and name badge, which read *Richard*, bore the logo of the security company that had installed the doorbell camera when Makenna and Zion first moved in. He was a hefty man whose overworked belt deserved a pay raise. He wheezed as he picked up his tool bag.

A toothy smile sprouted from his bushy moustache. He exchanged an eager, calloused handshake. "Good morning, ma'am. I'm here to upgrade you to our full security package?"

"Yes. Thank you."

They introduced themselves, and Makenna welcomed Richard in. He complimented her on the home's décor, modern without ruining the old farmhouse's charm. She thanked him and showed him where she wanted three new cameras installed. One was going in the living room, peering through to the kitchen. A second one was going in the upstairs hallway, guarding all three bedroom doors. A third one would overlook the back entrance.

Richard nodded. "Seems sensible. You've thought this through."

She had, but not for reasons she wanted to explain. The sleepwalking had become a regular pattern, a childhood habit resurrected by her stress. Even when she didn't wake up in Angeline's room or on the first floor, she found evidence she had been active during the night—or at least someone had been. She had considered putting the upstairs camera in her bedroom, to record what she was doing while asleep, but that was too violating. The hallway would have to suffice.

She needed to confirm *she* was the one opening cabinets, going through the refrigerator, and saving new pictures of Angeline to her phone's wallpaper. The alternative explanation was ... well, crazy, but whenever Makenna woke from her overnight wanderings, she had the sense she wasn't alone, that her hand was holding more than air, and that Angeline's hair had brushed against her cheek. It felt as though she were being led.

It couldn't be Angeline pulling Makenna out of bed to play with her or communicate, right? That kind of thing only happened in movies. Besides, Angeline had been a wonderful girl. No one deserved a perfect afterlife more than her. She wasn't guilty of anything, and she didn't have any grudges, the usual explanations people gave for hauntings.

After mounting the camera on the living room wall, Richard descended his stepladder. The stiffness in his joints was obvious. Fortunately, Makenna's own pain and swelling were healing well, but her injured leg had prevented her from jogging during the past week.

Richard pulled a tablet out of his bag and brought up the video feed from the camera. He toggled between regular and night vision. "This stuff has come a long ways since I started this work," he said. Richard was an exhausting conversationalist. While installing the camera, he had been recounting all sorts of stories and dumping endless questions on Makenna. "These cameras are getting smarter every day, and the internet makes it way more convenient to check what's going on. They're getting to the point where they can recognize dangers as they're developing instead of just recording robberies and disasters. I had a customer whose system noticed smoke and alerted him that he had a fire spreading before the detector ever picked it up. He grabbed an extinguisher and saved his house. Another customer was alerted when her son was choking. Good stuff."

"Mm-hmm." Makenna hugged her belly. She felt awkward observing the man's every action. She would have preferred to excuse herself to her bedroom, but she couldn't while a stranger was in her home.

Richard turned while on one knee and looked up at her. "You live alone?"

Makenna moved her hands defensively to her shoulders.

Richard scratched his belly. "Oh, I don't mean it like that. I'm an old man, happily married for over thirty years. I was asking because we can adjust system settings to better suit your family's needs. Got any kids?"

"I did."

Richard's smile shrunk from the coldness of Makenna's response. "Oh ... oh! Ma'am, I'm so sorry." He got back to work and, for the first time, left Makenna to the abuse of her own thoughts.

She curled onto the couch, leaning heavily on one arm rest, staring out at the pond. On cloudy days, the pond was as black as the period at the end of a sentence. She recalled happier days, when Angeline ran and played around its rim. Makenna watched the memories with crystal clarity, no haziness or fading.

What if these new cameras were unnecessary? What if recent scares were all in her head? Had she been seeing her grief instead of a ghost?

A light curl of worry tickled the back of Makenna's neck and brushed her hair. Makenna rubbed away the sensation.

"There you go," Richard said, hauling himself to a standing position. He carried several tools to his bag in the kitchen. "Try the app and let me know if the picture comes through."

Makenna navigated through her phone. Her security app now had two boxes on the home screen. One read *FRONT DOOR*, the other *LIVING ROOM*. She selected the latter. "Do I have to set it to night vision at night?"

"Nope, switches automatically."

She rubbed her neck again, more firmly this time. A ceiling-level view of the home's interior appeared on screen, with Makenna and the living room to the right, Richard to the left, unpacking another camera in the kitchen. "It looks good. Thank you." Something about the view bothered her, though. Tension compressed like springs in her back and legs, ready to launch her. The temperature plunged. What was out of place?

Subtle movement drew her attention to her neck. Shadowy fingers pulled away from her skin and ducked behind the couch.

A shotgun blast went off inside her. Makenna whirled to look over the back of the couch. "Did you ...?"

"Did I what?" Richard asked, coming into the living room both in person and on camera.

Makenna jerked her head around like a nervous bird. The only thing behind her was the hardwood floor.

"Ma'am?" Richard's expression tightened into concern.

"Can you pull up the recording of this room?" she asked, more urgently than she meant to.

"Not yet, but I'll make sure that's working before I go."

Makenna waited until Richard carried his toolbox to the back porch. She then got down on all fours behind the couch.

She checked the three-inch gap beneath it—nothing was there except breeding dust bunnies. Now it was the mystery touching her neck, making hairs stand on end.

***

Makenna fast-forwarded through hours of motionless, black-and-white recordings of her living room. For the first time, she understood her grandmother's old phrase, "A watched pot duh'int boil." Makenna had remained in bed the last few nights, so she hadn't emerged on any of the camera views, sleepwalking or otherwise. Angeline hadn't made her presence known either, but Makenna needed to check the footage, just in case.

Maybe there was a way to get Angeline's attention. She thought about what had worked on her daughter while she was alive ... chocolate chip cookies, fresh from the oven. They had been her favorite. Angeline would dance in the kitchen while the cookies cooled to an edible temperature. On more than one occasion, Makenna had used the treats as a bartering chip to convince her daughter to pick up her toys.

Later that day, she made the drive to town. At the grocery store, she dropped chocolate chips into her cart, but her attention was on the other end of the aisle. A mother was reading ingredients on the back of a box. Her young son, who was seated in the cart with their groceries, thrust a smartphone up at her, showing off cartoon images.

"Look, Mom."

"Uh-huh," the mother said flatly while returning the box to the shelf and selecting another.

"Mom, look at game! Look!"

"I am."

"No, Mom, look!"

You're not looking, Makenna thought.

"Mom. Mom. Look."

The mother slapped the box to her thigh. "What, Xavier? Yes, that's very nice."

"I can make him jump," the boy said, unfazed.

"Yes, good job."

Makenna steered her cart through a U-turn and moved on to the next item on her list. She wanted to shake that mother by the shoulders, to demand she set down that stupid box and enjoy whatever her son was showing her like it was a priceless piece of art.

Near the dairy aisle, Makenna's phone vibrated. She took it from her purse and, with a skip of excitement, pressed the *Motion Detected* message on the screen.

The view from her doorbell appeared. Angeline was peering into the lens just like she used to. She was smudged and slightly faded, a photograph damaged by water, but it was definitely her.

"You've been gone a while," Angeline said ... *that voice*! Her voice was like hearing music for the first time in a decade.

Makenna quickened her pace, steering her cart around an old woman. "I'll be back soon, baby. I just went to the grocery store for a bit."

"You're coming home after that? You're okay?"

"I'm okay, and I have good news. I'm gonna bake you a big, ol' batch of cookies."

"Yay!" Angline gave the slightest, cutest applause, but the excitement in her voice was much greater. "I love cookies." She hurried down the porch steps and skipped like she used to down the path.

Makenna brought the phone close to her mouth. "Angeline, stay away from the pond!"

The little girl's course bent, and she wandered down the road, out of the camera's frame.

Crash! Makenna's cart clipped a display in the middle of the aisle. Several jars of pie filling rained to the floor and burst. Every customer within sight stopped to observe her. Makenna's instincts told her she needed to fix the mess, to ask for paper towels or a mop, but there wasn't time. She pushed her cart through the widening puddle of fruit and broken glass and headed for the registers.

***

Water woke Makenna with a kiss to her forehead, then to her foot. Her first thought was her roof had a leak, but she quickly realized there was no roof, only grasping tree branches and a sky paved with black clouds. The drops had the coppery smell of a coming hard rain. They ganged up and chased Makenna to the shelter of the porch, where she lifted her damp pajamas off her shoulders and let air inside. The hissing weather grew louder, and rain curtains made the road and the pond beyond impossible to see.

Makenna faced the door. She had sleepwalked outside. How long ago?

Inside, she found a home reshuffled, with throw pillows thrown, a blanket draped over the back of the couch, and Angeline's stuffed cheetah ... her cheetah dropped heartlessly on the floor. Dishes were moved, a glass was half-filled with water, and the plate on the table had crumbs where one of the chocolate chip cookies had been.

Makenna's heart added thunder to the rain. She needed her phone the way a vampire needed blood. She clawed up the stairs, threw herself onto her bed, and felt her bedside table. The phone was missing. Makenna checked under the table. She turned on the light and reached into the gap between the bed and wall. Nothing.

She returned to the living room and kitchen, but a ravenous search achieved nothing more than misplacing more of her stuff. Yet again, Zion's absence was deepening her troubles. If only he were there, he could have called her phone and helped her locate it. How could he have done this to her, left her alone to suffer this nightmare? Had he been there on that horrible night, he might have been the one to interrupt Angeline's fatal trip outside.

Makenna checked the refrigerator in case she had left the phone in there ... sleepwalks were weird that way. That effort did nothing but waste more time. Makenna slammed the door, launching a landslide of groceries inside. She growled and barely held back a scream. "Where is my phone?"

A ring came from upstairs.

Makenna was terrified to move, then cautious, then rushing toward the noise. The ringing paused, then started again. It led her into Angeline's room, where a rectangle glowed behind the girl's pillow. The journey across the room was long enough for Makenna to ask a thousand stomach-churning questions, and none prepared her for what she found.

The identity of the caller was Angeline.

"Hello, baby?" Makenna said into the phone. "Baby, are you there?"

"You're awake." It was Angeline's sweet voice. Her muffled, haunting voice. "I worried about you being outside."

"I think I was sleepwalking."

"You were, but I made sure you were safe. It'll be okay, Mama."

Makenna heard giggles, both through the phone and from downstairs. Angeline hung up, and the time of the disconnected call blinked. The room was pitch black compared to that screen.

A message popped up. *Motion Detected.* Makenna pressed the first of multiple recordings that appeared. It was from the upstairs security camera, almost an hour ago. Makenna, unconscious, zombie-walked from her bedroom to the hallway, one hand held slightly forward of her hip. The space around her hand distorted. It pinched inward, wrinkled, and bristled with static. The video clip dimmed and brightened, dimmed and brightened as if it had a heartbeat of shadows. The recorded version of Makenna moved offscreen with the static, headed for the stairs.

The awake Makenna selected a later clip, skipping a block of time. Her knees turned into chewed gum, and she sank backwards onto the bed. Joy and terror rolled like dice in her chest.

The video clip came from the living room camera. Makenna was standing at the entrance to the kitchen. Angeline stood beside her, holding Makenna's hand. They didn't go anywhere, just wavered in place. After a few seconds, Angeline slowly turned and looked into the camera. Her identity was undeniable. There was Makenna's daughter, back from the grave, drilling into the camera with her pupils.

Angeline smiled and seemed to mouth the word, "Mama."

The clip ended, crashing the security app. When Makenna reopened it, all recordings from that night were gone, but she didn't need to see more. The sight of her and the ghost of her daughter, standing hand-in-hand, was permanently seared into her memory.

"Are you feeling better, Mama?" asked a giggling Angeline from somewhere downstairs. As expected, she vanished by the time Makenna hurried down there, and Makenna was unsure what she felt. What emotion described the most wonderful and terrible things being brought together as one?

***

Makenna's mind melted into the white spaces between the lines and letters on the computer screen. Her thoughts scattered like static. What was Angeline up to, she wondered? How could she help her daughter?

"Makenna, when can you have those budget updates?"

The question from Makenna's boss poked her back to reality. The shapes in front of her reformed into data. Her coworkers were on the other end of the conference call, awaiting her reply.

"Uh, tomorrow ... or Thursday at the absolute latest if problems come up. Do you need it in a presentation too, or just a report?"

"A report's good enough."

"I'd like some slides to show my team if it wouldn't be too much," said Avery, a manager from another department.

Of course, Avery had to make the task more complicated. Makenna vented frustration by tugging an invisible noose around her neck, and then she slumped forward on her couch. It was for moments like these that she kept the camera off during conference calls.

"*He-he-he.*" A giggle came from upstairs, followed by the sound of feet on wood flooring. Makenna peered up through the ceiling.

"Well, if no one else has any concerns," Makenna's boss said, "I'll speak to you all later. As always, feel free to shoot me an email if questions arise—"

Makenna disconnected and listened for more activity upstairs. She thought she heard another laugh. "Angeline, can you hear me?"

A pause, and then a faint, "Yes, Mama. I love you. Don't hurt yourself."

"I won't." Makenna cocked her head. "Can you come downstairs? I want to see you."

A pause, then, "Okay."

Makenna watched the bottom of the stairs and listened for the tattletale creak of feet on old steps, but that was a sound from the old Angeline. There came only silence. Makenna waited nonetheless, and her anticipation was rewarded with the sensation of a presence approaching her, filling her, and passing through. In the wake of the momentary encounter, the hairs on her body were left standing, and the room cooled.

"Angeline?"

"I see you, Mama," Angeline said through the camera perched on the wall. "You look pretty, Mama."

They were speaking. *They were speaking*. They were speaking!

Makenna stayed almost motionless. She didn't want to chase this moment away like a small bird. "Thank you, baby. I'm glad you can see me, but I want to see you too."

"Look at your phone."

Makenna brought up the security app. The living room view was centered on her, but she wasn't alone. A foggy, mishappened little girl was seated on the floor, knees held in her arms, back against the wall. The camera struggled to show her. That edge of the video feed flickered and darkened. When Makenna looked up from the screen, the floor was bare, but that didn't mean no one was there. They were so close ... so close ... but separated by infinity.

"That's not what I mean," Makenna said into her phone. "I want to see the real you, not a picture of you. Can I do that?"

Angeline rubbed her chin, pondering. "No."

"Why not?"

"It doesn't work that way."

"What do you mean? Baby, I want nothing more than to hold and kiss you. I want to spend forever with you."

"You can't do that. You have to stay here. Stay alive."

"I'm not going anywhere, but I want to see you again with my own eyes."

Angeline rose like a flower unfurling to the sun. She opened her arms in a pretend hug. "Can I show you something to help you feel better?"

"Anything, baby."

"Okay, but don't eliminate the files like Daddy this time, or you won't see the special surprise." Her warning was stern but tender, almost paternalistic. So mature. It was a reminder Angeline had been a brilliant little girl with a bright future.

"I promise. Show me what you want."

"Check your computer. Don't be upset, Mama. You were there for me, and that's why I'll always love you."

With that, Angeline walked off-screen, toward the door. A second later, footsteps could be heard outside, fading to separation.

Makenna felt like she was being throttled by a broken-down carnival ride. She walked to the space where Angeline had been, hugged the void, kissed the emptiness on the forehead. She then took a seat at the kitchen table, where her computer was again filling up with video clips from the day of Angeline's death. She had told officers she heard her daughter moving about the house at one o'clock AM. Makenna had groggily said, "Go back to bed," before returning to sleep. Those were her last words. Not, "I love you," but an annoyed, inattentive command.

She opened the file with 0100 in its name and let the video play. It was a pale, night-vision view of the porch, its banister, and the steps. An insect flickered briefly. A faint blush of light from the nearest town, miles away, marked the horizon. The furthest part of the stone path was dim, pointing toward the subtle glimmer that was the pond reflecting moonlight.

Nothing occurred in the first clip or the second, but in the third, Makenna heard a muffled suggestion of Angeline's voice. She turned up the volume. More mumbles, and then, "Where are we going?" The screen door clipped the edge of the video as it swung open. Angeline's wonderfully poofy hair entered the frame, followed by the rest of her, and then ...

And then Makenna was walking outside beside her, holding her hand. She wondered how she could have blacked out such a major detail from that night, but the answer presented itself. Makenna was zombie-lurching next to her daughter, the telltale movements of sleepwalking. They travelled awkwardly together down the fading path, sinking into the inky night.

Makenna's mind was an inferno of confusion. How could no one have mentioned this? When that clip ended, she immediately advanced to the next one. Every black pixel was under a microscope. Had the freckles of reflected moonlight on the pond moved? Was that pale speck video distortion, or was it Makenna's blue pajamas at a distance?

If she stared any harder at the computer, the screen would crack from the pressure.

Minutes after the two of them vanished, a specter formed at the farthest reach of the night-vision. It hovered unsteadily, then wandered around the road before ending up on the stone path. It was Makenna, head lowered in sleep, hands hanging empty next to her hips. Without looking up, she managed to reach the door and headed inside. The lock clicked.

Makenna skipped ahead several hours, praying for a happy ending she knew deep down was not coming. A bird sang into the microphone, warning of the coming dawn and tragic revelation. Makenna reemerged on the porch, now fearfully awake, calling her missing daughter.

At the kitchen table, present-day Makenna dried her eyes with her sleeves. She had a question she didn't want to ask, but like a mouthful of sour milk, she had to spit it out. "Angeline, why'd you go in the water that night?"

"You brought me there, Mama. We went together, but I didn't come back."

The reply, which came from the living room camera, disemboweled Makenna. Her entire understanding of that night dropped at terminal velocity and impacted like a meteor. The horror ripped away her grasp on consciousness. Makenna fell into a different kind of sleep, and darkness exploded from within. She blacked out before hitting the floor.

***

"Hello?" Zion asked.

Makenna squeezed her phone in both hands and beat it against her forehead. What was she supposed to say to that man?

"Makenna, is that you?" Zion said over the phone. "Hello? Did you call me by accident?"

"How could you, Zion?" What she really meant was, "*How could I*?" but she unloaded her vitriol at him.

"What do you mean?" He matched her aggression with defensiveness. "You're gonna have to explain because I have no idea what this is about."

"You said you deleted the footage of Angeline that night because there wasn't anything to see."

"Yeah, that's right. Why relive it?"

"How come you never told me it showed Angeline's killer?"

"What?" A chair scraped on Zion's end of the call. "Who'd you see? What did I miss?"

Wrong response. She could have strangled him. "Don't play dumb with me, you bastard! I saw what you hid!"

"This is crazy talk, Kenna." That was his nickname for her. "What are you on about?"

"The recordings, Zion! I ..." There were screws in her throat. "I drowned Angeline when I was sleepwalking ... and you've been hiding that!"

Zion was quiet. It was a confession. She was certain she had caught him ... but Zion eventually said, "Oh my god, you've absolutely lost it. That didn't happen. Why are you making this up, huh?"

"Don't tell me that. I saw it with my own two eyes in the video."

"Stop it! I saw the videos too. That. Didn't. Happen. The cops also watched them. Don't you think they'd have arrested you if—"

"Yes, I did!" The truth was excruciating enough on its own. She couldn't bear the lies and cover-ups anymore. Makenna dug her fingernails into the jugular of the air in front of her. "I know what I saw. I went with her to the pond and came back alo—"

"No. No. She went alone—"

"Zion, stop."

"No, you stop!"

"I'm not stopping till I get the truth out of you."

"You're making this bullshit up to victimize yourself instead of letting it go. You weren't in the videos with her. Leave me alone, because I don't want any part in this insanity."

Makenna brought the phone to her mouth, close enough to bite it. She screamed, almost reaching the same volume she had achieved when the police found Angeline's body. Hanging up took several tries because of how badly she was shaking, and then she dropped the phone and held her face. The phone cartwheeled off the edge of the table and clattered to the ground, where it soon vibrated. Makenna parted her fingers and peered down at the device, which was now glowing.

Motion Detected.

THE MYSTERY BOX

1
November 10, 2:42 PM
Present Day

I take my seat in a small conference room with no windows or artwork. The lighting is dim, and cameras are watching me like a hawk.

Sara Jeong joins me at the table. She's petite with short, black hair, attractive but professional, dressed in a teal skirt suit. Ms. Jeong looks to be in her late thirties like me, but make-up may be hiding a few years. During my tour of Doppeltech, she has exhibited cautious enthusiasm rather than bombast, so she's likely a mid-level manager at best. The big, arrogant fish stayed out at sea.

She gestures to the third member at our table. "What do you think, Detective?"

"What am I supposed to think?" I ask of the animatronic mannequin. Its face is an oval, digital display. The oversized anime eyes blink consistently but wrongly, like the tick of a clock that's slightly out of sync. Lines of black pixels representing a mouth bend into a quaint smile. Contours on the screen make vague suggestions of a nose and ears, and the scalp is a white plastic dome with visible screw slots. "It looks to me like you guys developed quite the expensive doll."

"Expensive, yes. Doll, no. No pull-strings are required to make her chat. She's fully conversational."

I place my tablet computer in front of them and blatantly press record. No sense in hiding it. Ms. Jeong has been seemingly open and honest with me so far. I might as well show her the same courtesy. "The robot is a she?"

"Or him. The unit is ungendered by default, but she's currently set to communicate like a college-educated, middle class, West Coast, white, American woman, so 'she.'"

The robot's anime eyes slide in Ms. Jeong's direction, then zip back to me with a cartoonish blur.

"All of those settings are adjustable in real-time," Ms. Jeong says, "and she could replicate your voice and speech patterns within seconds if you wanted her to."

"I'll pass on that, thank you." I lay my notebook and pen next to the recording tablet. Ms. Jeong gives this a strange look. "I like to keep some old-fashioned backups in place. Can you please explain why we're here, in this room? I was promised an interview with an expert from the SEVRR project. Instead, I get a preview of a Disney attraction."

"I assure you, she understands her own technology better than anyone on my team. You wanted to know what our predictive systems are capable of, Detective. She's a physical interface to the same SEVRR system you've been using, and that technological connection allows her to communicate at a near-sentient level. It gives her more than just a big vocabulary. She has a deep comprehension of human behavior, allowing her to interpret your reactions and respond in ways that best advance a conversation. It's similar to how you and I interact with others. If you wanted a peek inside the black box, this is your best shot."

I write "Black Box?" in my notebook. The mannequin laps this up with eyes that feel less cartoonish and more judgmental by the second. "You mean like on an airplane?"

"No, 'black box' is a term for a system with unknown internal processes. All we have are the inputs, the outputs, and a general sense of how it works." Ms. Jeong says this matter-of-factly, but operating something this powerful without understanding it seems like an obvious, terrifying vulnerability. She reads my concern and adds, "Don't worry, just because the inner workings are a mystery doesn't mean it's not controlled or regulated. Sometimes we're blind to a device's internals because the hardware or software is proprietary and owned by another company. In the case of predictive intelligence systems, however, it's because the data is processed on neural networks closer to a human brain than a traditional computer. The deductions account for countless variables or patterns too complex for us to recognize at a practical rate. That capability is a good thing. In the medical field, it's made it possible for doctors to identify cancer cells before imaging systems can spot them."

Ms. Jeong flutters her fingers. "Think of it this way. You drove here this afternoon. If I asked how your brain managed that, you'd explain that it used inputs like your eyesight and sent outputs to your hands and feet, but you wouldn't be able to explain *how* your brain physically processes those signals. No one can, not completely, but we trust those outputs all the same. The human mind is a black box, and so is any computed system emulating it."

I circle "Black Box" twice to remind myself to further research it on my own. "Hmm. That's ... a good example of why I went into criminal investigation instead of engineering. If I'm hearing you correctly, this only reinforces the concerns that brought me here in the first place. If SEVRR's inner workings are a mystery, how do you know when the outputs are mistakes? If the system tells me a suspect is 99% likely to commit murder, how do I know that's accurate and not the results of a typo in the code?"

Ms. Jeong tents her hands in front of her lips, then says, "We could get into a long, technical conversation, but it's better if I simply show you. Gnosis, please introduce yourself?"

"Gnosis?" I ask.

The dots making up the robot's mouth separate and come together like moving lips. The robot tilts its head in sync with its speech but in an exaggerated manner, like a cheerleader or a kindergarten teacher trying to engage their audience. "Good afternoon, Detective. I'm Gnosis, a physical interface for Doppeltech's Societal Evaluation and Violence Reduction Resource, or SEVRR for short."

She does sound like a West Coast white woman. Scarcely a hint of digital artificiality. "She only speaks when spoken to? How very 20th century."

"That's not actually one of my design constraints," Gnosis says. "Given the investigative nature of your visit, silence on my part was both prudent and polite. However, if I do have one thing in common with the women of the last century to whom you're referring, it's that my silence should not be interpreted as a lack of intellect. Choosing the time to speak is as much a matter of wisdom and social decorum as choosing what to say."

I feel flushed, like I've been reprimanded by a teacher who caught me cheating off a friend's test. "I'm sorry, I won't make that mistake twice."

"There's no need to apologize. Would you like to introduce yourself?"

"I'm Detective Grazer of the New York State Police Crime Prevention Division. How are you?"

"Good, thank you. I'm delighted to be speaking with you."

I squint, and the anime eyes do the same. "Delighted? Do you know what it's like to experience delight?"

"I could give an academic explanation based on publicly available research, but I doubt that's the intent of your inquiry. You want to know if I'm capable of feeling emotions like a human. In short, no, as that is beyond the capabilities of current artificial intelligence. Emotion is one of several characteristics central to the debate of sentience within digital constructs."

Ms. Jeong is beaming in the corner of my eye. "Isn't she incredible?"

"Yeah, but I'm now even more conflicted about SEVRR. I like it better when it's just a search bar on the computers at the station. Gnosis, you mentioned the 'nature of my visit.' Could you please explain what you think my purpose for being here is?"

The anime eyes always blink right before Gnosis speaks. There's nothing practical about it, so it must be a subtle detail meant to humanize her. "You're here to gather information because of a concern that SEVRR's system caused the death of an innocent victim."

2
October 19th, 8:54 PM
Three weeks ago

I sprint across the courtyard and throw my back against the apartment building, relying on the cushion of my bullet-proof vest. My pistol clips my bodycam as I raise it to my shoulder.

My partner, Santiago, catches up seconds later, huffing and wheezing. The round-cheeked, gray-haired detective is a senior member of our division, and he was my mentor when I first joined the force fifteen years prior. Back then, we tracked down kidnapping victims and caught hitmen, but now we work to prevent violent crimes.

Santiago whispers, “I don’t like that you’re spending more time in the gym. It makes it hard for an old man to keep up.”

“If you came with me, you wouldn’t be sucking wind right now,” I say.

“Meh, I’ll be done with street work in six months. It’s my time to fatten up.”

“Then stand in front of me and provide cover.”

“Har-har. You’re a comedian.”

The four members of NYPD SWAT Bravo Team are with us at the building’s rear fire door. They’re primed like thoroughbreds at the starting blocks. The moment Bravo Leader hears over his radio, “Alpha Team has reached the lobby,” he swipes his badge on the door’s electronic panel. Because we have a warrant and clearance for this intervention, the lock clicks open, and the fire alarm temporarily deactivates. Seconds later, Santiago and I are in the center of a six-man caterpillar moving up the stairs. Bravo Leader keeps his rifle trained on the next landing ahead of us.

My adrenaline's in fifth gear, but not out of fear for myself. These kinds of interventions have become routine, and the odds of the suspect having noticed us are slim. His family members are the ones in real danger. The suspect, a fifteen-year-old male named Ryan Taniv, has threatened online to kill them. The kid's school records indicate his main areas of study are fighting and getting suspended. His father's out of the picture, locked up for drug and robbery charges, but the suspect lives with his mother and her boyfriend, who's as familiar with the law as the biological dad. Worst of all, Ryan has three younger siblings, ages eleven, five, and two.

On the third floor, Alpha and Bravo Teams merge from opposite ends of the hall toward Apartment 315. Two civilians are in the corridor. One, a man taking a puff from his vape, goes wide-eyed and quietly shuts himself behind his door. The other is a woman carrying a laundry basket. Unfortunately, before likewise vanishing into an apartment, she screams as if the guns are intended for her. She's now raised an alarm for everyone in earshot.

Our ten-man force takes positions around 315.

"Condor," Alpha Leader whispers into his radio, calling the sniper across the street. "Alpha and Bravo are in position. Do you still have visual?"

"Condor, here," comes the reply over the radios. "Suspect has returned to the kitchen with his two youngest siblings. It looks like something spooked him. He's now looking around and yelling at the younger kids."

"Probably heard the civvie who screamed in the hallway," Alpha Leader says.

This is my moment. I had led the oversight on the suspect, analyzing all evidence provided to us by SEVRR. Ryan Taniv is calculated to be a 97.7% risk to others and himself. I'm playing the role of good cop, the one to invite him to a peaceful conversation down at the station. His apartment will be scoured for weapons, of course, and his family's life is about to get jostled like a tea party in an earthquake, but it beats dealing with another mass shooting or murder-suicide. No one wants another headline about kids becoming killers.

I put my pistol away and prepare to knock when Condor's voice comes in loud over the radios.

"Status red! Suspect has a gun! I repeat, suspect has a gun in proximity to his siblings!"

Alpha Leader shoves me out of the way and swipes his badge on the door's lock. "Go hot!" Eight men in black armor and black helmets burst into the apartment, moving like twin vipers into the living room. Santiago and I follow on their heels. We trample dirty clothes, bottles, and drug paraphernalia as we move.

A kid screams and dives to the left—the eleven-year-old boy. One SWAT member puts his knee on the kid's back, not to hurt him but to shield him and keep him out of the way. The rest of the force spreads out. The men bark orders, and children yell.

By the time I round the corner to the kitchen, Ryan is ducking behind his five-year-old sister to avoid the mean end of two rifles. His AR-15E briefly points at the girl's back—and I hold my breath—but the teenager darts deeper into the apartment. A door slams shut.

The youngest children are now bawling. SWAT quickly isolates them. I follow the remaining gunners, who pair up around several closed doors. “Condor,” Bravo Leader calls into his radio. “Do you have visual on the suspect?”

“Yeah, he’s in the kids’ room, crouched behind a dresser. Still no sign of adults. Be aware, suspect has his gun.”

“Roger. Stay locked.”

“Let me try.” I step up to the door, which is pockmarked with half-peeled stickers of cartoon characters. Bravo Leader eyes me. His expression, barely visible behind his dark visor, is equal portions caution and disagreement, but he sidles beside me rather than interfering.

My glimpse of Ryan had been briefer than brief, but what I had seen was normal terror from a regular kid. I’ve watched enough godforsaken footage of active shooters to recognize the demonic look those people adopt once they give in to the rage and take others down with them to hell. It doesn’t feel like we’re there yet with this boy. We still have a chance for a happyish ending.

The men behind me wrap fingers around triggers. I knock. “Ryan, it’s Detective Grazer of the New York State Police. We’re here to talk to you, but we need you to put the gun down first.”

“I didn’t do nothing,” comes the reply from the thinly paneled door.

“I know, and that’s why we just want to talk.”

I bargain for a minute or two before the kid gives verbal confirmation he’ll cooperate. He promises he’s laid down his rifle, but when I open the door, the weapon is still in Ryan’s hand.

In that moment, time slows. Minutes’ worth of thought fits into a fraction of a second. Ryan’s wielding the rifle more like a baseball bat than a gun. It’s the posture a person takes when they’re trying to scare off a robber, not murder someone. His finger's close to the trigger guard, though, close enough to escalate the situation. I also read the kid's soul, written in bold font in his eyes. Ryan is violent and defiant, yes, but he's also panicked and well-aware he's in over his head. He's the kind of kid who likes to talk big game and intimidate others—but it all screams, "Help me, I'm scared of life." We've intervened before he's gone beyond the brink, but I don't see a kid with a brink in the first place. Ryan is all bark and snarl, no bite.

But in a careless, poor decision, he starts to offer me his gun in a way that looks like he's taking aim. Across the street, Condor reacts. The window explodes—simultaneously, Ryan's skull does the same. A red crown erupts sideways from the kid's head. A flash goes off in my mind as my memory takes a permanent picture of that frightened boy's life spraying onto his unmade bed.

3
Present Day

"Could you please explain what you think my purpose for being here is?"

The anime eyes always blink right before Gnosis speaks. There's nothing practical about it, so it must be a subtle detail meant to humanize her. "You're here to gather information because of a concern that SEVRR's system caused the death of an innocent victim." In a hum of moving mechanical parts, Gnosis puts a finger to its cheek, another quirk meant to blur the line between robot and human. "It's strange you would wait until now to inquire about this, Detective. I have reliably guided your force for eighty-three months."

"*Has* it been reliable?" I ask. "You notice a few odd purchases and a few dumb comments from a teenager on the internet, and you decide that someone needs to get taken down? How do we know the difference between a threat that's 2% safe or 5% safe? And regardless of the rating, if he's the exception, that person is one-hundred-percent innocent and shouldn't be hurt. Making the right call doesn't always mean playing the odds."

"You likely heard that slogan from individuals protesting my incorporation," Gnosis says. "Is your position influenced by them? That kind of external interference is potentially a conflict of interest."

"Hearing other points of view isn't a conflict of interest, especially when they've raised legitimate concerns." It's a good thing I brought my own pen instead of a cheap one from the department, because it would have snapped by now from how tightly I'm squeezing it. I know it would be entirely meaningless, but part of me wants Gnosis to apologize for Ryan Taniv's death. "People are still innocent until proven guilty."

"That ideal has never been successfully maintained by humans in their court systems. Why should that be the standard now?" Gnosis says this like a lawyer who's been waiting for the right moment to deliver a prepared rebuttal. "The government must assume a level of guilt among their citizens before committing resources to prevent criminal activity, otherwise it would not be a reasonable use of funds and energy."

I scratch an abbreviated version of that statement into my notebook so I can look up the source later. "Is your position also influenced by others, or whatever nonsense? You didn't come up with that argument by yourself? Where'd you hear it from?"

"From no single source. It was a projection of what best to say based on statistical analysis of effective communicators." Gnosis leans forward. The eyes are androgynous, emotionless, but the voice is trying to be motherly and comforting. "Detective, it must be stated, humans have traditionally mistrusted statistical arguments because they struggle to reconcile individual biases, uncertainties, and misinformation. Optimal solutions are often ignored when falsehoods or selfish reasons present more compelling motivations. My accumulative intelligence algorithms correct for flaws of the individual, and yet my results are judged by those same individuals."

"You're right, people are flawed," I say. "You'll get no argument from me there. But since when is the truth reached by taking the average of those flaws?"

Gnosis's pixelated mouth shifts from left to right. "My analytical capabilities are more robust than that, but they cannot account for errors humans make when acting upon my recommendations. I did not choose to shoot a child you perceived to be innocent ... a human did that."

4
October 20th, 11:20 AM
Three weeks ago

Santiago is wrestling me out of the captain's office. His grip moves from an assertive hand on my shoulder to a demanding arm around my gut. "Let it go, kid." That term of endearment is a coded message. It was his general nickname for me when I started out in the force, but now he saves it for moments when he disagrees with me. It translates to, *I like you, Oliver Grazer, but you're wrong this time, so shut up.*

I don't make it easy for Santiago to extricate me, nor do I avert my attention from our scowling captain. "Who was operating as Condor yesterday? Who pulled the trigger?"

Captain McHenry had already been in a sore mood when I burst into his office. Now he's ready to chew me up and spit me out. "It'll be in the report when SEVRR releases it. Until then, you're hardly in a state to demand that information. There's enough violence out there, I don't need my officers brawling in here too. Good day, Grazer."

I grip the door frame, straining against Santiago. "That boy should be in a counselor's office right now, not on a coroner's table. I was supposed to have a chance to talk to Ryan—"

Captain McHenry's fists hit the desk and launch him out of his seat like rocket boosters. "That suspect had a goddamned gun pointed at you, Grazer! I'd expect you to protect your badge brothers and sisters under the same circumstances, otherwise we end up with two body bags instead of one. Good lord, you're throwing fits when you should be thankful to be alive. No, I'm not telling you who Condor was. Santiago, get him out of here and cool him down."

"You heard 'em, kid." Santiagio uses his second hand to grab my shirt collar.

I level a finger at Captain McHenry. "This isn't justice. Sweeping this under the rug just means more kids will get shot."

"Out, Grazer!"

The door slams shut as Santiago corrals me to our perpendicular desks. Everyone in our office has become a spectator to my outburst, but I threaten them with a glare to mind their own business. Rather than trying to work and pretend nothing's wrong, I snatch up my coat.

"Where are you going?" Santiago asks.

"Home. I'll fill out my report from there. The captain wants me to cool off."

Santiago nods. "Is the wife home?"

"Probably," I say, "but the bourbon definitely is."

"They're both good ways to vent some steam and take a load off the mind."

My laugh is nothing more than a puff of sarcasm. "Sure."

"Things still choppy between you and Molly?"

I don my coat with emphasis. After a pause to weigh possible understatements, I say, "We're not exactly newlyweds. Ups and downs are gonna happen."

"Still, she's a good gal, and it'll be better to fix what's broken than to later regret not trying. Listen, this job will rip you apart if it gets its fingernails under your skin. Shit happens. That thing with the boy yesterday? I agree, it's a tragedy. Maybe he didn't deserve the outcome, or maybe we intervened barely in time, but either way, he and his family made a lot of bad choices that led to what happened. You don't own this. You gotta swallow it with a bit of sugar, or something stronger, and keep going."

"Noted," I say as I slip my laptop into my bag and head for the exit.

"I'm serious, Grazer," he calls after me. "I've seen other good officers and detectives lose their cool after particularly rough cases. I don't want to see another."

The commute to Staten Island is quicker than usual because most people are headed into the city than out this time of day. The southbound lanes of the Chisholm Bridge are practically empty.

My phone chimes with a text from Jenny, the girl who delivers food from Molly's favorite gyro shop. I know what the message is without reading it. Jenny, who weighs maybe a hundred pounds wet, is asking me and my wife to put our overly friendly golden retriever inside so she doesn't get tackled—a lesson learned through experience. Molly has apparently ordered lunch for herself.

Sure enough, Jenny is backing out of the driveway when I arrive. She rolls down her window to greet me. Jenny has straight, black hair like Gothic curtains, but her grin could fry a vampire. She is sunshine personified, and I don't know how much of her enthusiasm I can take in my current state.

"Mornin', Mr. Grazer. Beautiful day, ain't it?"

"Yeah, good weather."

"It's *wayzo* warm for October. I hope it keeps up so I can wear the costume I got for Halloween."

"I hope so too."

"I brought a treat for Marlowe," she says, referring to my dog. "I slipped it to him through the door while dropping off the food."

I ease off the brake and let my vehicle creep toward the driveway. "Thank you. Sorry, but I'm in a bit of a hurry."

"No problem. Enjoy lunch."

Molly's bike is parked inside our condo's single-car garage, further proof she hasn't left for work yet. As I enter the home, Marlowe greets me like a fur battering ram, then bounds around the first floor, barking to announce my arrival. I drop my bag in the kitchen and swing both doors of the liquor cabinet wide open. Molly's food order is on top of the cabinet and makes the air smell good enough to eat. There are two boxes instead of one. Huh ... I didn't tell her I was coming home.

Molly enters the room with a phone to her ear. Her smile melts at the sight of me. Freshly showered or bathed, she's wearing a robe and a towel around her head.

"You're home early," she says. "I wasn't expecting you."

The liquor is suddenly less interesting. "You must have been expecting somebody if you came in here with a grin." I don't hide the fact I'm questioning her robe. Why would there be two lunch boxes? And is that perfume I smell?

"I gotta go," Molly says into the phone before hanging up. She then squares up with me, arms crossed. "Don't be like that. Of course I figured it was you, I'm just surprised by the time. What's your problem?"

"Nothing." I point a thumb at her delivery order. "Who's the second one for?"

"Me, unless you really want it. I couldn't decide between gyro salad and orzo soup. One's for later."

The Dalwhinnie whiskey is singing a siren song. I poke my head back into the liquor cabinet but keep Molly in the corner of my eye. "I came home because I can do my work from here, and someone at the station was pissing me off."

"Real impressive, Oliver," she says sarcastically. "You came in at two AM last night with alcohol on your breath, waking me up, and now you leave work early to day-drink. Way to reach for the stars with your life goals."

"Well, excuse me for working a job with real stress. We can't all teach meditation."

Molly doesn't know about the incident with Ryan Taniv, nor that I had spent an hour in my parked car after the shooting, using music and darkness to wash the blood stains out of my memory. I don't tell her everything I deal with, firstly because marriage isn't clearance to hear every private detail from my cases, but also because she tends to spread salt with the balm. God gifted Molly with plenty of good qualities, some of which she keeps in shape as an exercise instructor, but whenever she tries to console me, I end up lower than where I started. That's truer than ever after nine years of marriage, time enough for Molly's eyesight to dim to all but my worst traits. Experience has taught me I'm better off alone in my own head than getting advice from my spouse.

I want this conversation to end before it gains the momentum of a fight, but Molly persists. "If you have an issue with a coworker, you need to man up, go to your captain, and work it out between the three of you. It's the only way to resolve it, and it's certainly better than embracing alcoholism."

"Having a drink is not the same thing as alcoholism."

"Did your dad make the same excuses before your mom had to kick him out?"

"I don't know, Mol. Ask your boyfriend on the phone. Better to be drinking alcohol than spritzing up to meet someone when your spouse is away. Sorry I spoiled whatever your plans were."

"It was my sister on the phone, you ass. Projecting much?"

"You love acting defensive for someone with nothing to hide."

"Because no one likes having false accusations thrown at them. You're making assumptions, Oliver. Sometimes your gut is wrong."

I don't meet Molly's eyes. Instead, I slam dunk two ice cubes into a glass and open the whiskey. The malt and peat are incense to cover the stink of our marriage of late. The arguments had crept in slowly over little things I can no longer remember, but neither of us has been willing to throw in the towel.

"Where *were* you last night?" Molly asks, brandishing her own accusation.

I keep the whiskey bottle tipped for more than a single serving. "Trying to do my job, and screwing it up." I pop the last word like it's a balloon in my mouth.

Molly looks like she's struggling to bite her tongue. She takes her exit. "I'm not doing this, not when you're gonna act like a child. Don't take things out on me all because other people are making you unhappy."

"Noted."

I isolate myself in our office. Before getting on my laptop and typing a scathing account of how SWAT handled the intervention, I check the search history on the computer my wife and I share. Have there been any searches for restaurants, bars, or other places Molly might meet her "sister?" I don't see any evidence, but that doesn't mean my intuition is wrong.

5
Present Day

Gnosis's pixelated mouth shifts from left to right. "My analytical capabilities are more robust than that, but they cannot account for errors humans make when acting upon my recommendations. I did not choose to shoot a child you perceived to be innocent ... a human did that."

That comment stabs under my sternum and drives me back in my seat. I drop my pen into the gulley of my notebook's open spine. It's then I escape the tunnel vision of my conversation and remember Ms. Sara Jeong is still in the room.

"Did you tell it that?" I ask. "What has Doppeltech been digging up?"

My reaction catches Jeong off guard. She crosses her arms defensively. "Nothing, I promise. I'm not sure what the two of you are talking about."

"I never confirmed the shooting victim of my investigation is a child."

"She's telling you the truth." Gnosis continues to smile with fizzy, fake enthusiasm, but its voice stumbles into colder, harsher tones. Logical. Paternalistic. Accusatory. Aloof. "The details of your case were recorded in SEVRR by multiple parties, of which I am an interface. As for knowing this is the situation that brought you here, that can be inferred based upon your internet searches and conversations you've had within proximity of cell phones."

I stop Gnosis with a raised palm. "You wiretapped me?"

Ms. Jeong considers her words before responding. “No, Detective. Doppeltech has exclusively operated within the boundaries of the law. This is the same broadnet technology application used to screen all potential threats, and for decades, search engine companies have used similar strategies for marketing. No one is listening to your conversations or reading your internet activity because that would require nine billion employees to keep track of nine billion different users. Instead, Gnosis screens for telltale patterns in internet traffic, data that would be noise to you and me. Only after an entity presents themself as a likely threat is the data retroactively used to determine the suspect’s identity, and it’s then the authorities are notified. As long as a person isn’t giving off red flags, they’re invisible to the searches.”

“Then why am I on the watch list?”

Gnosis bends into a surprising, exaggerated posture, one closer to a willowy damsel. “Detective, I pulled that information in real-time as we spoke. The data is readily available, and my observations do not exclude people in law enforcement. If they did, the public would be at a significant power imbalance and vulnerable to exploitation.”

“Are there people who are excluded from broadnet data mining? Doppeltech executives, for example?”

“That information is proprietary and not within the legal parameters of your investigation.”

“Thank you, I can read well enough between the lines ... You said suspects are identified and targeted after they’ve given enough hints to suggest they’re a threat. Who sets and reviews those thresholds?”

Gnosis blinks. “Law enforcement officials do so after we present them with evidence.”

"But who's checking if it should get sent to us in the first place?"

"In the interest of protecting Doppeltech intellectual property and profitability, that information is also proprietary, and you would require legal authorization to review it. You would not likely find anything of value in that review, however. As Ms. Jeong explained, my comprehension is continually improved by iterative learning. It replicates organic brains, making evaluation of my thought processes nearly impossible."

"Right, right, the black box and all that."

Regardless of how Doppeltech wants to spin the situation, they've been spying on me. Like everyone, I know tech companies snoop through my cellphone, but right now it feels like the paparazzi is in my pocket, straining to overhear my conversation. I drop my phone on the table. "Can you show me how to turn off the spying functions? The private details from my cases shouldn't be stolen and used for profit. Police have to get warrants for that kind of info."

The dots making up Gnosis's mouth roll in a wave that somehow feels sarcastic. "Detective, you misunderstand the situation if you think that will have much effect. The world is full of electronic ears, and I'm connected to all of them."

6
October 29th, 2:28 PM
Two weeks ago

A hand slides a paper coffee cup next to my keyboard. I look up from my computer screen to Santiago, who has a coffee of his own.

"You look like you could use some caffeine," he says. "How's the evaluation of the Robertson suspect going?"

"Slow." Santiago is referring to one of our current investigations, a guy whose recent unemployment and gun purchases have put him on the watchlist. I don't want to tell Santiago that for the last few hours, I've been in a Gabbit internet forum, anonymously discussing the Ryan Taniv incident with people who have turned it into conspiracy theories. The most popular one is that police murdered the kid to intimidate his family and prevent them from going public with the NYPD's dirty laundry.

Those accusations are useless word clutter. The real reason I'm on the forum is a user named BoneWhistle14. This individual is wisely questioning SEVRR's role in Taniv's death, and they've also identified four other minors who were questionably shot before they could—supposedly—commit horrific crimes. BoneWhistle14 is arguing the claims are a convenient way to hide mistakes by police officers, but the jaded peanut gallery in the forum is more than happy to write good riddance to the deceased.

Gotta disarm time bombs before they go off.

Boohoohoo another dead white boy stopped before he can murder everybody why stop at 1?

NYPD removing another carbon footprint. Overall win.

Too bad the kid and the cops didn't pull the triggers at the same time.

I'm tempted to unload on all the little bastards hiding behind usernames, but I'll only be rewarding them with attention. BoneWhistle14 is ignoring those commenters as well. Instead, they're chatting with users who want to understand the risks SEVRR poses to the general public.

BoneWhistle14: You only hear about obvious mistakes in the news. What's worse are the ones you don't hear about because no one knows SEVRR's involved in those.

This isn't an average lunatic or troll. They're logical.

"Captain says he doesn't want you on field responses for the time being," Santiago says from his desk. "Doesn't trust your mental balance after the Taniv thing."

"Yup," I say as I search the forum for more posts by BoneWhistle14.

"Why didn't you tell me?"

"Only found out this morning myself. It's good news for you because it means you also get to sit them out."

"Yeah, but I don't want to ride off into the sunset like this. You need to smooth things out with him before you get a new partner, otherwise he'll assign you someone like Patel."

Every single officer in the city knows that's the last pairing you want. Patel is a migraine disguised as a detective.

BoneWhistle14: I know it's suspiciously convenient for me to claim this, but I can't reveal everything I know online.

Poketoker: The risks with SEVRR are theoretically significant, but what tangible examples do you have? Can you at least hint at the cases?

BoneWhistle14: There are a few big-name people involved

you would recognize, but writing them would bring us all unwanted attention. SEVRR uses more than just the police for its dirty work. Suffice to say, it's a good way to quietly deal with opposition if you're a high enough official.

Santiago swears into his coffee cup. "That Robertson guy's driving near his old employer. I'm gonna message spare units in the area to hang close and keep an eye out."

I grumble, "The guy also grocery shops and picks up his kids from school in that same neighborhood. It's probably no big deal."

"SEVRR says the violence risk is high."

"Screw SEVRR. Roberston lives in a rough neighborhood, hence the gun, and after losing his job, he traded in a more dangerous weapon for a cheaper one and some cash. You don't do that if you're out for revenge. I'm skeptical it's time for panic bells."

"Still, protocol says we put eyes on his likely targets and protect them."

"Protocol's a convenient scapegoat for bad ideas."

Santiago begins typing, ignoring my gripes. "What's gotten into you, Grazer? Listen, I've been dealing with groups of murdered kids since you were a youngster yourself. I'm tired of the wanton violence, and this computer system is the first thing that's put a dent in the number of shooting incidents. You're throwing out literal babies because of one bad bath water."

"Fine, go ahe—" A comment in the Gabbit forum bulges out at me.

BoneWhiste14: Look into Trent Cavender. He was an ex-Doppeltech employee whose car crashed after he started working with protestors and the media.

Trent Cavender? I haven't heard of him, but a bit of internet dancing brings up someone who died three years ago when his vehicle took a tumble in the Rocky Mountains. The death was investigated as a possible self-driving malfunction but later deemed a suicide.

Santiago claps once. "Patrol caught Robertson on failure to come to a full stop. They're checking his vehicle for the gun. Oliver, you want to review their findings, or me?"

"You got this one," I say as I type a message to BoneWhistle14. Maybe there's a way we can talk in person, if they're willing.

7
Present Day

The dots making up Gnosis's mouth roll in a wave that somehow feels sarcastic. "Detective, you misunderstand the situation if you think that will have much effect. The world is full of electronic ears, and I'm connected to all of them."

Internally, I'm reeling over this brazen admission. Sure, Big Brother is everywhere, but this room is apparently where he lives. Everyone knows being born in the 21st century means having little choice but to submit to the voyeuristic gawking of advertisers and government agencies if you want a cell phone and internet access. SEVRR is an evolution of what already existed and is far from a secret. Doppeltech sold it to the public as a necessary means to combat gun violence, and as a user of SEVRR, I know better than most how deep its fingers reach. Still ... this peek at Oz behind the curtain makes the boogeyman real.

My mouth is suddenly dry. Ms. Jeong hasn't offered me a drink the entire time I've been here. "Cellphones? Security cameras? Computers? You're saying you're tied into all of them?"

"Those are the common options, yes," Gnosis says. "Almost every device with a microchip has a microphone. Internet usage is another valuable tool. If I can't access a suspect's local devices, I can read transmissions to and from servers they connect to. The process is swift. If I query you, for example, Detective, I find your full name is Oliver Steven Grazer, home address 1714 Oriole Street. Your last online purchase was a burrito from Señorita Salsa two hours ago. Your latest search in incognito mode was—"

"Stop!" The information feels like filthy hands groping at me. "None of this is relevant, and my personal information shouldn't be made public."

"It's not public. It's being revealed to you directly, Detective, and it's information you already know."

"We're not alone here, but that's beside the point. You're wasting processing on me when it's supposed to be focused on dangerous individuals."

Gnosis simulates a laugh. "It's no additional effort for me to pull this information. My processors are not at capacity. You desired to better understand my capabilities. This presentation is relevant to that goal."

Ms. Jeong shifts her seat closer to her robot. "You seem unsettled, Detective, but none of this should be a surprise. Without these capabilities, SEVRR would be unable to interdict criminals."

"Criminals *and* everyone else. Sorry if I sound spooked, it's just different hearing something like this used against yourself rather than a third party. During the early adoption of SEVRR, your company pitched it as a last resort invasion of privacy used only after a threat is confirmed."

"And we do that. Gnosis only did this as an exhibition." Ms. Jeong shakes her head like I'm a child struggling to read a simple word. "If we didn't broadly scrape data in real-time, then any response to a threat would come too late. There's nothing personal in that approach until someone has exhibited a dangerous pattern. I assure you, Gnosis doesn't hold onto secrets like a person does. Everything is ones and zeroes barring a dangerous signal. I understand your reticence, but this technology has been vetted by courts of law."

"Like I said, it's just different when the focus is on yourself."

The further I get into this conversation, the more eager I am to speak with BoneWhistle14 directly. What would they think of this?

8
November 8, 6:31 PM
Two Days Ago

My thumbs are sprinting through the last leg of an email on my phone when Molly enters the living room. She's adjusting her earring, and a sliver of purple skirt shows beneath her zippered coat. Our dog, Marlowe, circles her because he knows we're getting ready to leave.

Molly heads around to the backside of the couch, and my shoulders shrug in hopes of being massaged like they used to. Instead, she hovers.

"What?" I ask.

"C'mon, we need to go. My sister's birthday dinner is at seven. Be late for your own stuff."

"I'm done, see?"

She does see, quite intently. My phone is drawing her attention like a flame luring a moth. I tip the screen away from her, and there's a momentary void in our conversation that feels off, like she's waiting for a punchline to a joke I never said.

Minutes later, I back my car out of the garage. I've been anticipating this dinner all day. It's not that I particularly enjoy the company of my in-laws or faking how good things are between me and my wife, but I need an evening without work. In addition to my normal caseload, I've been investigating Doppeltech on my own time. They've agreed to speak with me and give me a tour of their facility in Connecticut. If I want to make the most of this opportunity and ask the right questions, I need to know their background like I know my own childhood.

Molly knows nothing of this coming interview, nor does Captain McHenry or Santiago. I'm well aware this Ryan Taniv case has become a personal obsession, but it sits with me like a hemorrhoid. The more I look into SEVRR, the darker the shadow it casts.

"I have to travel on Monday," I say as I drive.

Molly gives her lipstick a final inspection in the passenger-side mirror. She closes the visor with surprising swiftness. "Where are you travelling to?"

"Connecticut."

"Why?"

"It's work related." That answer bounces off her like a basketball off the front of a rim. "What?"

"I didn't say anything."

"It doesn't matter, I saw your reaction. You don't believe me. It's related to a case. I can't discuss it."

"Fine, it's for a case." Molly's bristling with skepticism. She digs a white envelope out of her purse. "Can you tell me what this is?"

"I have no idea. You tell me."

"It arrived by private courier today. It's addressed to you, but there's no return address. Who sent it?"

I glance at the label. It's printed ... no handwriting. "What's with the sudden interrogations? How should I know who sent it?"

"From a secret admirer?"

Molly is half-kidding, but the serious half is an oncoming tornado. I promptly swerve the car into an open parking spot along the curb. An SUV blares its horn as it swings around me.

"What are you doing?" Molly asks angrily.

"No, what are *you* doing?"

"Nothing! Can't you take a joke? I just wanted to know what this is."

"But you ask like *that*?"

"Like what?" Molly hands over the package by slapping it against my chest.

"Cripes, woman! What's gotten into you? Do you want to go to this party alone?"

"No, then everyone will be asking questions. Just drive."

Our fights have sharply escalated during recent weeks. It's been a few months since we've slept together, and the space between us in bed might as well be made of brick. Things haven't been this ugly since our engagement, when I messed up and Molly caught me drunkenly kissing another girl. Apologies weren't enough, and the marriage was called off, at least for a while.

Molly and I got back together a year later, but we both saw other people during the break, and that became ammunition during arguments. If I came home late with friends or coworkers, Molly wanted to know if I had been "friendly" with other women. I would play the Uno Reverse and ask if she'd seen her old boyfriend from the gym lately. His name was Cale—like the health food, but with a C—a guy with bronzed, Mediterranean skin and a shaved head as smooth as a fortune-teller's crystal ball.

Fortunately, things improved with time. The second year of our marriage felt like the true honeymoon phase, and for a while, things were good. There were the nights spent watching action or comedy movies together, which led to our own romantic stories on the couch. I followed her on hikes, and she acted so sweetly toward me at parties that guys in my unit teased me about it. We matured and stopped picking old scabs ... until recently. We both hate what we've become, but being the one to wave the white flag feels wrong, and I don't know why.

What's eating me is the instinctive certainty that Molly's keeping a secret. If this were a criminal case, my intuition would be enough reason to follow the lead. I get the sense she's looking for an escape route. I had recently suggested we visit a counselor, but she had rejected the idea, which is all the more reason to believe she wants the situation to deteriorate. Molly hates failing at anything, so it's possible she's waiting for me to withdraw or make a mistake, that way I'll be the one taking the blame if we separate. The SEVRR investigation couldn't have come at a worse time. My attention is divided when I should be fixing what's broken at home.

The envelope I've been given feels empty. I peel open the flap.

"I didn't seriously accuse you of anything," Molly says, "but you've been acting strange lately, and you're so absent."

Because I don't want another kid to die unnecessarily! I wish I could shout that at her.

"Overtime is nothing new," I say. "It comes with the job."

There's a single slip of paper in the envelope. It has an address in Pennsylvania followed by the message, *Detective Grazer, meet me Tuesday at noon if you wish to chat in person. Come alone. BoneWhistle14.*

I had been questioning this stranger for days in the Gabbit forum, wringing them for more details about SEVRR. They had refused to go deeper unless we meet in person, and the conversations stopped there. How did they get this message to me? I never revealed my name or address.

"The party's starting soon," Molly says.

I put the car into drive. At dinner, Molly and I play the role of a happy couple. It mostly works, though at one point, her mother asks if I'm all right. She's interrupted me while I'm contemplating BoneWhistle14's message. Whoever they are, they shouldn't have been able to track me down. Do I go through with the rendezvous? It's an obvious risk but a tempting one. I do know one thing, though. Given Molly's suspicions about my trip to Doppeltech, I'll be keeping this second excursion a secret.

9
Present Day

The further I get into this conversation, the more eager I am to speak with BoneWhistle14 directly. What would they think of this?

Ms. Jeong and Gnosis are resolute that broadnet data scraping is blind to individual identities unless necessary. Their answers haven't deflected my concern about innocent targets in the slightest. I steer the conversation back on track.

"Reset. Let me use an example to convey the problem. Picture the suspect. He's a kid who comes from a troubled home with access to guns. He has a history of violence, but only goes so far as fistfights with his peers. That background increases the likelihood that he'll become a school shooter, do you agree?"

"I would not call myself an expert in child psychology," Ms. Jeong says, "but I believe so."

"More importantly, do *you* think the child in this example presents an elevated level of danger?" I ask Gnosis.

"Undoubtedly, yes."

"Okay, but that background describes lots of kids, most of who don't become killers. And those kids should be allowed to grow up and live fruitful lives. Do you also agree with that?"

Ms. Jeong and Gnosis both answer in the affirmative.

"So, let's say you're me, a detective trying to prevent the next mass killing. You get an alert from SEVRR that this kid with a troubled past is suddenly high-risk and needs to be dealt with. What should you, as a detective, do?"

While Ms. Jeong weighs her response, Gnosis speaks. "To prevent loss of life, the suspect should be isolated from the public, and authorities should implement a correctional plan according to law."

"But in that process, as police officers try to apprehend the supposed suspect, one of them shoots the kid, and he dies. I, as the person overseeing the case, don't know if the shooting prevented the murder of a dozen kids, or if we've wrongfully killed someone who would have become a fine adult. How am I supposed to know if it was Situation A or Situation B?"

"Given the outcome," Gnosis says, "there are two non-exclusive possibilities. The suspect has acted in a problematic manner that brought the shooting upon themself, thus confirming they were a high-level threat. Also, the police procedures are flawed and should be addressed. Either way, SEVRR has served its intended purpose, and the issues are human ones that lie elsewhere."

"But I saw the kid with my own eyes, and my assessment, as someone who's been doing this job longer than a computer, is that SEVRR was *wrong*." I usually play the good cop, but I find myself leaning over the table at Gnosis. "Wrongful warnings endanger people. They make officers nervous and trigger-happy, which increases the likelihood of a tragic accident."

Gnosis absorbs my rising voice. The artificial blinks are an aggravating tic. "Your assessment is based upon far less data than is available to me, and as with all human judgments is vulnerable to error. Humans are adept liars and vulnerable to being affected by others' falsehoods."

"Machines can lie too," I insist.

"Machines do not lie. They perform tasks according to how they are programmed."

"You're splitting hairs. The tasks of those machines are still grounded by human programmers, people who lie, have ulterior motives, and make mistakes like everyone else. Convince me I'm the one who's mistaken and not the programmers who trained SEVRR."

For once, Gnosis pauses before replying. "Detective, you would undo the progress made in combatting gun violence over a hunch in one situation? That is not pragmatic. There remains a high probability your assessment of the suspect is simply wrong, which would make further investigations unnecessarily disruptive."

"Detective." Ms. Jeong cups her fingers as if remotely holding my hand to comfort me. "You seem to have negative assumptions about Doppeltech and our development staff."

"No, Ms. Jeong, it's just that my role requires me to be a pessimist of all individuals but an optimist for humanity in general. If questions don't get asked, people get hurt."

"I'm sorry this situation occurred, and Doppeltech takes your concerns seriously, but these circular hypotheticals could continue indefinitely. Our system was heavily scrutinized before receiving government approval, and it was held to highly stringent requirements. We've done everything possible to minimize risks. Realistically, those risks can never be *completely* irradicated, but we would argue, with evidence, that the current risks are preferable to those that existed before—"

My cellphone shivers noisily on the table. The screen illuminates with a text message. "Excuse me, one second." I take a quick peek at who's contacting me. It's probably a spam advertisement or a bill reminder. I worry it's Molly on an inquisition, trying to prove I lied about why I traveled out of state.

Instead, the message is from Jenny. I figure she's asking to have Marlowe put inside, but it's a strange time for that request. Molly should be leading an aerobics class right now. Why is she ordering food?

The text is sloppy in its grammar but precise in knocking the wind out of me.

im sorry if this upsets you Mr Grazer but i respect you so i think you should see this.

There's an image attached to the message. It's a distant snapshot of the front of our house. The number 1714 is visible on the maroon front door. What's also visible is Molly in the arms of a fit man with a shaved head. Their lips are locked, and her hand is glued to his bronzed cheek.

10
November 11th, 11:53 AM
One Day After the Gnosis Interview

It's been a five-hour drive to this small Pennsylvania town, and I've struggled to breathe the entire time. My body's a roulette wheel circling through cold, black anger and white-hot despair. It's hard to focus on the road when all I can see is that picture of Molly kissing Cale. The distraction nearly causes me to miss my exit, and in my overreaction, the car's collision avoidance system is the only thing that saves me from side-swiping a truck in the next lane.

Last night, I stayed at a hotel, partly because I drank too much at a bar to drive, and partly because I wasn't sure how I would respond to Molly. I need time to strategize. How do I drop the evidence on her? Do I want to hear a confession, or am I dreading it?

A car horn barks at my rear bumper, and a construction worker emphatically swings his arm to get my attention. I'd failed to notice traffic is moving again. Road signs indicate I'm on Main Street in this old, industrial town, but the location is a construction zone of apocalyptic proportions. Buildings to the south have been bulldozed, and the sidewalks are being jack-hammered to add lanes for a parkway. The brick buildings on the north side of the road are getting plastered with dust and noise. The newly opened acreage is a fenced-in plot of mud and gravel where girders stick up from the ground like steel crops. Best guess, the town is getting a Walmart and a car dealership.

After the chain-link corridors and traffic cone obstacle course, I turn left down a road shouldered with tree stumps. The path is cratered like the surface of the moon. It runs for only a quarter mile before it's dammed up by a raised highway. There, in that pocket of nothingness, sits a solitary white RV.

The lawn décor is as aesthetic as the surroundings. A sun-bleached lawn chair sulks next to a foldable table with an abandoned mug on top. The fire pit is a repurposed automobile wheel. A tipped-over plastic snowman lies face-down in the weedy grass. I would assume I'm in the wrong place if not for the items mounted on the RV, which include multiple antennas on the roof, bars on the windows, and an array of spotlights and cameras. Whoever's inside is not keen on visitors.

"Hello?" I shout after getting out of my car.

The RV door opens, and a bearded white male of about thirty emerges. He's dressed in a baggy sweatshirt and sweatpants with pockets large enough for a gun, but judging by his movements, I don't think he's packing. He has posterboards tucked under one arm. The man waits for me to break the ice.

"Hi, I'm Detec—"

The man slaps a finger to his lips, ordering silence. He then shows me the first of the posterboards. It reads *Leave your phone in the car.* This is definitely BoneWhistle14 or someone associated with them. Anyone who spends their time prophesying about the evils of SEVRR and government spying would undoubtedly not want cellphones leeching off our conversation. My recent interview of Gnosis has me interpreting his precaution as wisdom rather than paranoia. I've been seeing its ghosts in everything that runs on electricity.

I feed my cellphone to my car's glove box. When I raise my head, BoneWhistle14 is holding a new sign that reads *Any other electronics*? I shake my head. His third sign insists *No weapons*. To that, I show him the sidearm holstered under my jacket.

"That one's gonna be a problem," I say. "I have less reason to trust you than for you to trust me. You already know I'm law enforcement. The gun stays with me."

The man considers this for a few seconds before bobbing his head back-and-forth. "Fine, fine, come inside." He has a low, crackly voice that probably doesn't get a lot of exercise.

He holds the door to his RV open. As I climb inside, I point to one of the cameras. The eyes and ears of Gnosis are everywhere. "Aren't those an issue?"

"They're on my own closed system, and I inspected their components before installing them. The internet has no idea they exist, so we're fine."

The man has the mannerisms of a mongoose, smooth but quick. The interior of his home, which has a bachelor's musk, is ten economic brackets above the haggard lawn. His computer has a monitor that was a movie theater screen in its previous life, and eight different web pages are open at once. A second screen shows the feeds from the exterior cameras. The furniture is weirdly shaped, a modern artist's lucid dream. A cursory glance at his gold-label liquor cabinet has me hopeful he'll offer a drink of something I could never afford.

"Your computer's on the internet, right?" I ask.

"Of course, but that doesn't mean I haven't taken safety measures. I'm not an idiot, Detective."

"Didn't say you were."

The man drops into his desk chair and lets it rotate thirty degrees to the right. He sits like a soggy, oversized pair of underwear. His legs splay wide. BoneWhistel14 pulls a vape out of his pocket, takes a hit, and exhales the scent of weed. "Shoot it straight. Tell me how familiar you are with SEVVR's capabilities."

"I'd say I'm quite familiar. I've been using it for a while, and yesterday I met Gnosis."

His lips tighten into an *Oh, really?* expression.

"May I have a seat?"

He gestures to the dining table, which has seating for two, but all signs point to this guy living alone. "I was one of SEVRR's designers," he says. "Gnosis was in the draft phase back then. Did they waste funds making it into an animatronic?"

I nod. "For what it's worth, it was impressive. I'm guessing that experience with SEVRR is what gave you the know-how to hack me and figure out my real name and address?"

"It's not hacking. I didn't break into anything. It's a matter of knowing where to find information. You don't actually think a VPN and a few pseudonyms make you anonymous on the internet, do you?"

I was already bothered this guy had dug up my personal details, but his bristly attitude is going to make it exceptionally difficult to bite my tongue. "I'm also not an idiot, sir."

"Hopefully not. Yeah, I utilized the same channels as Gnosis to locate you, but it's far more efficient at it. No human could ever keep up."

"I suppose that experience also helps you keep a low profile, right?"

"I wouldn't be alive if it didn't." He reads my skepticism. "You think I'm exaggerating. I'm not a nut. I wouldn't have chosen this lifestyle if it wasn't necessary. In fact, if I had known you'd already spoken to Gnosis, I wouldn't have risked meeting you. Visibility spreads like the flu."

"Why did you invite me here?" I ask.

"Based on your questions, I thought you might be with the press. Finding out you're law enforcement is even better. It's one step closer to putting people behind bars." He chews the tip of his thumb. "It's really bothersome you met with Doppeltech. I guess it's not the end of the world, but still ... it's a good thing I planned on relocating soon."

I peek through the barred window at the construction vehicles assembling a warehouse-sized structure. "You pick this spot for the incredible scenery or the price?"

"Neither. I chose it to sell. Home addresses of detectives aren't the only thing you can find online if you know what you're doing. You can also find out which sites are being surveyed by corporations looking to expand. Swoop in, buy the property off a private owner, and then sell it at a markup when the company comes knocking."

Molly briefly pops into mind. I'm feeling antsy. I stand and move about the RV's interior, taking note of artifacts from BoneWhistle14's past. There's a framed photograph of California redwoods. It's likely a picture he took himself, so he's at least traveled the West Coast, but there's also a good chance he worked in Doppeltech's Silicon Valley branch for a while. "Stealing corporate expansion plans certainly sounds rather illegal. Why confess to a guy with a badge?"

"Are you all that concerned about companies getting outplayed on real estate?" he asks.

"No, not really. Do you have a name you're willing to share, or do I call you Bone?"

"Trent."

"Like Trent Cavender, the Doppeltech employee you told me to investigate?"

He rolls his vape between his fingers. "I am that Trent."

That raises my eyebrows. "You're supposed to be dead."

"Funny, that. An old friend needed a truck for a while, so I let him rent mine off me. This was around the time I left Doppeltech on a sour note, threatening to expose them. Wouldn't you know it, but a little while later, my truck gets inspired and decides it wants to be a bird. On a perfectly clear day with no weather, it careens off a cliff while my buddy is driving through the Rocky Mountains. I suspected Doppeltech hacked the self-driving function, which they're capable of doing, I just didn't think they'd stoop so low and attempt murder. I needed them to think they succeeded, so I accessed my friend's dental records and made sure they looked an awful lot like mine. It worked. Trent Cavender was reported dead, and my friend got relegated to the missing persons list."

My hunch has been validated. All this time, I suspected Doppeltech was hiding dirty laundry, but I didn't think the case would take this dark of a turn. "What's your end game in all this?"

The ex-Doppeltech employee crosses his legs and immediately uncrosses them. "To see my attempted murderers arrested so I don't have to hide. But more than that, I'd like safeguards imposed on SEVRR, which was one of my recurring arguments with them back then. I left the project because they ignored my design recommendations. Doppeltech is protective of their cash cow. They won't limit it unless they have no choice."

Trent and I share what brought us to this moment. I describe the Ryan Taniv killing in basic details. In return, Trent discusses his history with Doppeltech, and my notebook gains a list of executives that ought to be investigated. Behind the scenes, the company struggled to eliminate bugs, some which may still plague SEVRR. One notable issue was a tendency for SEVRR to artificially boost risk assessments when repeatedly queried about the same suspect. The resulting self-fulfilling prophecies meant moderate threats becoming high risks simply due to being tracked.

He notices my interest in his whiskey collection, and he offers me a glass of aged Macallan. The bottle is probably worth more than my whole day's salary. While he pours, he names several congressmen with deep connections to Doppeltech.

The Macallan is exquisite. "Which tree do I bark up first?" I ask. "The politicians, or the company execs?"

"Both. Tech money is always a hydra with lots of heads. The people in charge cover for each other so long as the profits flow. You need to turn the public against them and SEVRR, and unfortunately that requires sacrificial lambs like this kid you told me about. Theoretical dangers are too easy to accept. There needs to be blood and sob stories before humans demand change."

His use of the word *humans* strikes me as odd and removed. It makes him sound like Gnosis.

Trent types in a Gabbit thread while he talks, gesturing to my reflection in his monitor. "It's like with automated driving. To make a change, you're going to have to go against people's natural tendencies to be lazy. When vehicles got collision-avoidance systems, it did reduce major accidents as intended, but do you know what else happened? Drivers' capabilities atrophied and minor accidents went up. There were more mental mistakes because drivers weren't focused, and they relied on sensors that were only meant to be an added layer of protection. We love offloading our responsibilities onto automated systems, so much so that we don't care if it's making people behind the wheel more dangerous. That's where you are with SEVRR.

It's *easier* to let someone else fix gun violence with computers than for us to all fix ourselves. Humans need to care about the innocent victims and, more importantly, worry about becoming the next victim before they'll reconsider the easy solution. We're selfish that way."

"All due respect, Trent, but that sounds like the kind of evangelizing you've been doing online, and I don't exactly see angry masses gathering outside Doppeltech's door. I'm a realist. I can sniff out wrongdoings and deal with criminals, but I'm not your guy if you want to change the minds of millions."

Trent sighs and rubs the bridge of his nose. "I'm not asking you to lead a revolution, I'm asking you to support it."

I let a chuckle slip. "Isn't *revolution* a bit of a strong term, Comrade Lenin?"

Trent shoves his keyboard across his desk like a toddler refusing a plate of vegetables. He crosses his arms and spins his seat toward me. "No, it isn't, because a counter-revolution is already being waged against us. SEVRR isn't only a crime-fighting tool, it's the brain behind all sorts of applications, and not enough of us are asking how we'll change for the worse due to handing over the wheel to a computer. It's maddening how nonchalant people are about this. *'Oh, a kid got shot because the computer system made a mistake? Aww, shucks. A teenage girl killed herself because a creep took her picture on the subway and generated it into a porn video right then and there? I sure would be upset with that app if it wasn't so good at turning my face into a cartoon dog. What's that, SEVRR's AI core is writing children's books too? I can't see this having any negative repercussions, even though* Mein Kampf, Lolita, *and* A Clockwork Orange *are mixed into the training data. What life lessons will an amoral machine teach our future psychopaths? Can't wait to find out.'"*

He's breathless after his rant. I pry my way back into the conversation with a question. "If this all bothers you so much, why did you work for Doppeltech? SEVRR exists in part because of you."

His reaction could generously be called a slight twinge of guilt. He takes a quick pull from his vape. "We had a saying. 'Better the devil who cares than the devil who doesn't.' I tried to put safeguards in place, but in every battle between money and safety, money won. The people with real power were only concerned with staying ahead of the competition, cut corners be damned. Naïve me eventually gave up on them doing the right thing, and now I'm Frankenstein trying to kill his monster."

"I don't see how this will work, though. I can't actually prove the kid we shot wouldn't have killed someone else, and the other officers want me to let it go. You can't just broadcast the details to the public and expect them to demand SEVRR be shut down."

"You're right because this is the wrong case for framing the narrative. You need an innocent victim who got shot and survived or lost their job, so long as they're able to tell their own story. It's even better if they're a pretty girl from a middle-class family because the media will be all over that for the clicks. Find a martyr and pit their image against Doppeltech. I've only tracked a few instances, but there's got to be better candidates in the police databases."

"And from there you exploit the martyrs to prove SEVRR's lying?" I ask.

Trent wags his finger. "Machines don't lie. They don't even make mistakes, really? Not like people. At worst, computers make errors based on faulty designs and programming from developers."

I shrug. "That's basically the same thing, and it's the same thing to most people whose attention you're trying to get. If I do this and find your source of fuel, are you going to be the one lighting the fire?"

The LED on Trent's vape turns stoplight red as he takes another hit. He breathes the fumes toward the ceiling. "It'll be an inferno."

11
Present Day

There's an image attached to the message. It's a distant snapshot of the front of our house. The number 1714 is visible on the maroon front door. What's also visible is Molly in the arms of a fit man with a shaved head. Their lips are locked, and her hand is glued to his bronzed cheek.

"Are you okay?" Ms. Jeong asks.

I sniff and stiffen my face, wiping the emotional slate clean. It's a trick I learned in law enforcement, one I normally use before telling someone their loved one has died, that way I'm not the first one to cry. "Yeah, I'm ... it's okay."

How quickly can I drive home?

"You look unsettled."

I waggle my phone, but I don't show the screen. "Sorry. I was caught off guard by some bad news, but I'll be all right. It doesn't affect us."

"Your tone suggests you are affected," Gnosis says.

"Yeah, well ... bad news is bad news. Some of us understand that at more than an academic level. Let's cut to the core." It takes strength to stay focused on the talkative mannequin seated across from me. "You've been elusive with general questions, so let me be specific. The case that brought me here involved Ryan Taniv of Brooklyn, deceased October nineteenth of this year. Can you provide me with all evidence that elevated his threat level? Anything not included in his original reports."

"Access to that information would require legal clearance," Gnosis says. "In order to protect people's privacy, there are limits on what I'm allowed to share."

"Fine, I'll see if I can get clearance, which will waste time for all of us. Ryan was flagged because he had access to a firearm and made multiple concerning statements. According to the report, in one situation, his friend sang the lyrics, '*Bitches get a bop-bop*,' to which Ryan said, 'That's my mom, a bitch.' The song is about someone snapping and killing their girlfriend after she cheated." I swallow. "Are you familiar with the incident I'm presenting?"

"Yes," Gnosis says.

"There we go, some headway. This next question may throw you, but stay with me. Are you aware of other teenage boys who have made similar statements, *and* who also have weapons available to them, but who were dismissed as threats? Maybe these others quoted the same song as Ryan, or maybe they made similarly disturbing comments, but ultimately it was determined the threats were empty promises. Do you know anyone who fits that description?"

"Yes, I can identify many examples that match your description."

"What was it about Ryan that caused you to sound the alarm while other kids in similar situations were ignored? What made Ryan's situation worse? Make this make sense."

Gnosis holds a wide-eyed stare and says, "Detective, my report included multiple text messages Ryan sent to himself. In them, he complained he hated his family. As a human, did you not find them alarming?"

"'Alarming' is a strong word. I hate one of my cousins because they're the living embodiment of arrogance, but that doesn't mean I wish him harm. Ryan's texts read as typical teenage angst to me. It's a stretch to claim they're proof he was a killer-in-waiting."

"Those text messages indicate high risk when combined with his longer private writings."

"What writings? I wasn't made aware of this information earlier."

"It was filtered out in favor of information that is more relevant and usable in a court of law. In his other personal writings, he expressed a desire to harm his family, but they're in a notebook I cannot track."

"Wait, you mean like a diary or something?" I write *"Journal?"* in my notebook.

"Yes, he wrote gruesome stories in a red notebook not unlike yours. His mother confronted him about the writings not long before Ryan's life ended."

I cock my head. "How would SEVRR know what somebody wrote in a paper notebook?"

"I overheard the conversation between Ryan and his mother. She slapped him, and that led to a physical altercation."

12
November 11, 7:18 PM
One Day After the Gnosis Interview

"Please leave your message after the beep."

The robotic voice gives way to a brief tone. I set aside my troubles and put on a pleasant façade while leaving a message.

"Hi, Mrs. Taniv. This is Detective Grazer of the New York State Crime Prevention Division. I'm sorry to bother you, especially at this difficult time ... but I wondered if you could please give me a call. I have just a few questions. I promise no one is in trouble, and I'm hopeful this will bring some solace to you. Thank you."

I provide my phone number and hang up.

I'm parked down the block from my house with a vantage point of the front door. No bald scumbags have come or gone, but lights are on throughout the house, including the garage. Earlier, I swung by the gym and Cale's duplex, the address of which I looked up on the police database. There wasn't a plan to the excursion, I just needed to see the guy with my own eyes. Not surprisingly, he wasn't outside either location, so I eventually headed home.

I open my phone's contacts list and hover my thumb over Molly's smiling face. What's my play? If the gym rat is inside my home, a call will send him scurrying.

Instead, I text *I'll be home soon.* I then wait for the front door to burst open and for a half-clothed figure to emerge. Anger and testosterone are flowing through my veins like nitroglycerine. I don't care how much time he spends lifting weights, I can take him.

Molly replies to my message with a text of her own. *Don't bother.*

My brain slams the brakes with both feet on the pedal. So that's how it's going to be? She's so brazen in her cheating that she's willing to kick me out?

Her follow-up message reads, *I kno what yu did you bastard.*

The dam bursts, and I'm flooded with further messages.

I put your stufff in the garage.

Take it.

Im sure youll be happir sleeping somewhere else anhway.

My parents r flying out tomorrow. Dont be here when they arrive.

I'm a teakettle at full boil. I anticipated a lot of moves, but not this. Not for Molly to slap down the victim card and throw this situation in my face.

The drive to the house takes seconds. The garage door opens, but my headlights slam into a barricade of cardboard boxes and plastic bins. I can see clothes. Shirt sleeves hang out of one of the bins.

The door inside the garage swings aside. Marlowe bounds into the garage, excited by the sound of my car's engine. Molly also appears, arms crossed around a box. It's obvious by the color in and around her eyes that she's been crying, but at this moment, her expression is vinegar and knives.

We both rush to get in the first word, but it's a head-on collision of accusations. Marlowe cowers from the conflict. I try several times to mention Cale, but Molly's too busy shouting to listen. "Put it all in your car! I don't want any of it here."

"You're kicking me out of my own house?"

"Maybe you should have thought about that before screwing Danita, huh?"

Danita? That name tilts me off-balance. "Who's Danita?"

"That's what I'd *love* to know."

Lights go out in the neighbor's living room. They're listening and trying to be subtle about it.

Molly takes one hand off the beat-up cardboard box she's carrying and holds up her phone. "You messed up big time adding me to your sickening, little back-and-forth chat. '*I'm almost to Connecticut babe.*' '*Can't wait to see you again.*' '*Babe you were fantastic last night.*' I literally vomited while reading it. You're so disgusting. I knew ... I just *knew* ... things have been weird for a while, and, well ... yep, here it is."

The veins in Molly's face stick out like abandoned garden hoses. She flinches when I slap the top of the box wall.

"Wow," I say sarcastically. "I can't believe you. You're the reason things have been weird lately. I've been trying to fix this marriage, and you've been nothing but frigid."

"So, you go to this Danita?"

I'm pulling my hair. "There's no Danita! I don't know who you're talking about ... Wait, you're making this up to cover your own tracks."

"Bullshit. Don't bullshit me, you ..."

The tears are back, but I have no interest in consoling her. All the work I've done to put food on the table and keep our neighborhood safe means nothing to her. "Whoa, no, no, no. I see what's going on. Funny how you choose now to accuse me of wrongs, right when you go back to sleeping around with Cale."

Her jaw drops. "Really, Oliver? That was years ago. You're going to bring that up and try to claim what you did is fine because we're equal?"

"Not years ago." Where is the picture? I've pulled up the photos in my phone, but I don't see it. I'd forced myself to look at it at least a half-dozen times. It should be right here. "Yesterday. You had him over while I was gone."

"That's as insane as it is BS. Don't you dare try to turn this on me."

"I have evidence." I scroll through my messages. The conversation with Jenny should be one of the most recent ones. Where is it?

"I don't care what made-up evidence you have. Get out! Take your mail with you."

She heaves the beat-up cardboard box she's holding into the rest. I hear the clatter of metal pieces. The label on the box reads *OVERNIGHT.* Molly slams the door shut and locks herself inside the house. Marlowe is left in the garage, ears and tail lowered as he tries to figure out his alliances.

I want to throw open that door, barge inside, and see who else is in there, but something tells me I've already missed anything that might have happened. I kick one of the boxes before picking it up.

13
Present Day

"I overheard the conversation between Ryan and his mother. She slapped him, and that led to a physical altercation."

I nod at Gnosis. "Finally, something I can look into. What other proof do you have?"

Ms. Jeong fidgets. "Detective, please understand, this goes beyond the initial purpose of better understanding how SEVRR supports your department. If this is a test of our system's capabilities, I'll have to ask you to present your concerns formally. There are processes for that kind of evaluation, many of which, I'll remind you, have already been completed to verify SEVRR's reliability. You would need to work with the federal agencies that hold us to very strict standards, and I would need to have other managers and lawyers present."

"We don't need to go that far," I say. "No one is being charged with anything. If I have a better understanding of how the process works behind the curtains, I'll be better able to adjust how our department utilizes the data provided to us."

Gnosis blinks. "That information would also be relevant to someone who is attempting to have the program shut down."

14
November 12, 12:07 AM
Two Days After the Gnosis Interview

Half the lights are out in the sign of the Shooting Star Motel, making it look like I'm pulling into the parking lot of the Shoot Mo. I laugh because I read it as "Shoot Me" initially, which sounds like a splendid idea. What a hell of a night it's been.

Navigating the narrow parking lanes is a challenge, especially with several drinks down the hatch, but I manage to avoid scratching any other cars. A homeless man is leaning against a light pole at the far end of the lot. I hope he doesn't get any ideas about breaking into my car. My stuff is clearly visible in the back and passenger seats.

The woman at the motel's front desk is watching a video on her phone and munching on microwaved popcorn. I put my elbows on the counter, and she lets me know with loud-and-clear body language she's annoyed by the interruption. I probably look like the homeless man from outside. I'm carrying my possessions in cardboard instead of a suitcase, I haven't showered in almost twenty-four hours, and my breath is at least sixty-proof, but I don't care.

"Can I help you?" Her New York accent is thicker than motor oil.

"I need a room for the night ... Umm, two nights." I push my credit card and ID toward her.

The woman—her name badge reads Isabella—picks up the latter and feigns checking it. She then types at a computer and reads off the price for two nights. "Do you want breakfast? It's extra."

"No."

"K." Isabella swipes my card. She puckers her lips in a *that figures* fashion. "It's declined."

"How?"

"You tell me, but no card, no room."

My jaw's clenched enough to bite through steel. Molly must have locked the account. She's determined to be an absolute nightmare. I dig through my wallet for my backup card and, fortunately, it covers the bill.

I stumble into Room 132, which has a stale smell that matches the stains on the carpet and blankets. I unpack bare essentials, including liquor. A few drinks straight from the bottle makes my vision spongy and unsteady as I venture online for a while, searching for more information about Cale. It's not long before I drop onto one of the room's beds and fall asleep.

***

I have a lot of calls to make, and I'm going to have to do so while a hangover migraine is wedged between my eyes like an axe. I'm late for work, so I text Santiago to let him know I'll be in before lunch. I call the credit card company next. The labyrinthine menu options and castrated hold music wear my patience down to the bone. While I wait, I begin digging through the boxes I've brought into the motel room.

Eventually, a lady answers the call and takes my information. Her pleasant demeanor sounds artificially sweetened. Is she even a real person, or a bot?

"Your credit limit has been reached," the voice says.

I need a drink of water, both for my headache and the taste in my mouth. "How? It's supposed to have a thirty-thousand-dollar limit."

"Yes, and it was reached yesterday. You made a transfer of your remaining balance to another account."

Molly. What a spiteful monster hiding inside the woman I've been married to for years. "My wife must have done that. What am I supposed to do?"

"You're Oliver Grazer, right?" she asks.

"Yes."

"It wasn't your wife who made the transfer. Your name is on it."

"That wasn't me."

"We have signatures and audio agreements approving the transfer. This was done yesterday. Are you claiming this transaction was not facilitated by you?"

"Yes, obviously! Was my account hacked?"

"That's unlikely, but I can double-check." Why does the lady insist on maintaining her patronizing, sugary, southern charm? She should be upset alongside me. "Is it okay if I put you on hold?"

My phone vibrates. I check who's trying to reach me. "Yeah, put me on hold. I have another call anyway."

"Thank you."

I switch to the other call. The phone number matches that of Ryan Taniv's mother. I'd forgotten about her due to the whirlwind situation with Molly. "Hello, this is Detective Grazer. Is this Mrs. Taniv?"

"Yes." Her voice has been run through the belt sander of a lifetime of smoking. "I'm sorry I didn't return your call sooner. I ... was occupied."

"It's fine, Mrs. Taniv. You called at a good time. Listen, I've become aware of some additional information about Ryan. Are you willing to answer a couple questions?"

"I don't understand what it matters anymore."

"You have my assurance your family is not under investigation, and I may be able to improve the public's view of Ryan."

There's a pause before she timidly says, "What questions?"

"Thank you. I understand the two of you may have had altercations in the recent past. Physical ones?"

"Where'd you hear that?"

"That's not important, I only want to confirm the rumor."

One of the boxes in the motel room is the beaten-up one that Molly threw. The overnight label is addressed to me, but there's no return address, just like the message from Trent. I pick at its multiple layers of tape.

"We had some fights, yeah. Ryan was a teen, and I was his mom. It happens. He hit me one time, but I don't know how you know that."

I shake the package, which is fairly heavy. Metal rattles. Whatever's inside is broken, but the sound is familiar ... "Did he perhaps write about that in his journal?"

"What journal?"

"A red notebook he used as a journal. You confronted him about it after finding some disturbing writings. I was wondering if that were something you'd be willing to let me analyze."

"You're not making sense. My kid didn't have a journal. He wasn't the type to write, so I don't know who you've been talking to. Was it his father?"

Had I erred in my assessment of Ryan Taniv? He had been terrified when confronted, that much was certain, but was my gut leading me astray on everything else? If I was wrong about the journal, what else was I wrong about ...

I jerk upright quickly. My migraine shifts like a bag of marbles. The reason I thought Ryan had a journal was because Gnosis had claimed so. Had it been able to lie, despite Trent's claim to the contrary?

"Mister, I'm not okay with this conversation."

"I'm sorry, I was mistaken in what I was told. You have my condolences."

I hang up, and my phone returns to the call with the credit card company. The lady insists I authorized a balance transfer to another account and that I'll need to file a report on their website to challenge it.

"I'll have to do that later," I say. "Bye."

I drop my phone on the motel bed and stare like there's a tarantula crawling out of it. What had Trent once written? *SEVRR uses more than just the police for its dirty work.*

Had the comment about the journal been a misunderstanding. According to the news, generative AI still has a tendency to hallucinate, which is why people like me and Santiago have to review all data before proceeding with the apprehension of a suspect ... or was the comment about the journal intentionally misleading? Was it a red herring? And if Gnosis is intentionally leading me astray, what other steps might it take?

The credit card company thinks it received an audio agreement from me for the credit transfer, but Ms. Jeong had said SEVRR could emulate my voice within seconds of hearing me speak. The forged transfer occurred after I interviewed Gnosis. It was during the interview that Gnosis mentioned the journal for the first time. Did it hallucinate that detail?

What else hasn't fit during the past couple days? There was ... the photograph of Molly kissing Cale.

My insides wrench all at once. How could I have been such a fool? We both received texts or pictures of each other cheating. The ones she received are fake, so the one I received likely is too.

We're being played.

I have an itch to contact Trent and see how he would handle this, but he's hours away. I could reach out to him online, but that's worse. Also, can I trust him? He was SEVRR's designer and had connections to Doppeltech. Everything escalated after I contacted him. Can I trust he's telling the truth?

Jenny! I've known Jenny for a while, and she supposedly sent me the picture of Molly and Cale. She can confirm or deny it.

Despite wanting to avoid my phone as much as possible, I call her. I wonder if the voice on the other end will be hers, or an emulation of her?

Jenny doesn't answer. After one ring, a robot tells me, "This number has been disconnected."

"Is that your doing too?" I ask. Is SEVRR listening to me right now?

I next try calling the gyro shop where Jenny works. It's still early for lunch, but there are probably people on-site prepping for the day ahead. I get sent to voicemail twice, but on the third try, the shop's owner, Sal, picks up. He's understandably annoyed.

"Hi, whoever this is, we're not open. Call back later."

"Wait!" I say. No click. He's listening. "I'm sorry to bother you, but I need to speak with one of your employees. Her name is Jenny. It's urgent."

"Jenny don't work here no more," Sal says.

"What? Since when?"

"Since last night on account of what she's been posting online about us. She's been crapping on our reputation. None of it was true, mind you. That's not what this call is about, is it? I run a clean shop."

"No, it's not that. Thank you."

The timing of this can't be a coincidence. I've unfortunately pulled Jenny into my situation. I need to be careful, but I can't vanish off the radar like Trent. I could switch to someone else's phone as soon as possible ... that'll make me harder to trace. Who do I trust the most? My mother's in Texas, too far away to be of any help. There's Santiago. He'd willingly give me the shirt off his back, and right now, I need a whole lot more than a shirt.

Ultimately, I need to confront Doppeltech and stop whatever's going on.

I shower, and while I'm getting dressed, I cut open the mystery package so I can check it for bugging or tracking devices. Everything electronic is a potential ear for SEVRR. As I lift the box's lid, I finally recognize the metal tinkling sound, but that doesn't make the contents any less baffling.

It's a box full of ammunition, 40-caliber, the same as what my pistol uses.

"What the hell?" I say aloud. The curveballs I've been thrown are starting to make sense, but this one's a knuckleball.

15
Present Day

"If I have a better understanding of how the process works behind the curtains, I'll be better able to adjust how our department utilizes the data provided to us."

Gnosis blinks. "That information would also be relevant to someone who is attempting to have the program shut down."

"That's not what I'm suggesting," I say. "I think accidents will be easier to avoid if there's more transparency in the data you provide."

"That's something we can look into." Ms. Jeong rises from her seat. "I'll bring that suggestion up with my management team. I can also make sure you have the latest version of our user guide, but we're limited beyond that. I'm truly sorry if one of your investigations failed to completely avoid tragedy. We here at Doppeltech consider ourselves public servants like yourself, and we're doing everything in our power to protect citizens, including those who are a danger to themselves. I hope this presentation has been enlightening, though. Count yourself privileged, Detective. We've only recently begun showing off Gnosis and her capabilities. We anticipate an exciting year ahead."

I close my notebook, which is briefly tracked by Gnosis's gaze. "I wish I could say I'm leaving here with a warm and fuzzy feeling. May I email you if I have further questions?"

"Of course." Ms. Jeong considers her answer for a moment. "Well, within limits. My responsibilities do keep me busy, and some inquiries must be reviewed by the legal team before I can answer. It's that way for any company like ours."

"Yeah, par for the course. I look forward to those user guide updates. If I'm going to keep relying on SEVRR, I want to make sure it's completely safe."

"That's an illogical standard," Gnosis says.

Ms. Jeong tenses, like she wants to reach over and put a hand over Gnosis's speaker, but the robot continues before she can respond.

"Mass shootings are down 41% since my adoption, and previous human-dependent systems were prone to flaws and corruption. Law enforcement itself is susceptible to crime. Your own captain, McHenry, has dealt with witness tampering and evidence planting in your unit. Two of your old colleagues were arrested for illegal activities. If SEVRR is judged according to those standards, I represent a significant increase in public safety."

That cuts deep. Some of the worst moments in my career have involved arresting men I thought of as brothers, and once again, it's unsettling to hear Gnosis mention things that feel like they should be out of the computer's reach. "Well, I know it's a cliché, but not all cops are bad. My priority is guarding the innocent."

"So is mine," Gnosis says, "which puts us at an impasse if your efforts obstruct mine. The public is best served when we are on the same team."

"And if we're not?" I ask.

16
November 12, 1:01 PM
Two Days After the Gnosis Interview

As I emerge from the elevator, every officer stares at me like I'm a ghost. They know something I don't—actually, I can guess what's on their minds. The captain is going to skin me alive for going MIA. I'm a dead man walking.

Santiago doesn't say a word when I plop down at my computer, at least not initially. He scratches his chin as he surveys me, and then he grabs my coffee mug. "I'll fill this up. You're gonna need it for how late Captain will have you working tonight. Should I ask?"

"Yeah, but not here." I grab an envelope from my desk drawer and write, *Don't say anything, I'm having issues with SEVRR.* I then slide it toward Santiago.

He meets my caution halfway and whispers, "What do you mean, 'issues with SEVRR?'"

I put a finger to my lips to silence him. One of the officers notices and jokingly copies my gesture. I glare at him. I don't care if I'm becoming a madman like BoneWhistle14, the office is full of ears and eyes, and I'm not giving Gnosis any additional reasons to mess with me.

My next note reads *I investigated Doppeltech, and now I'm getting hacked.*

"Why would you do that?" Santiago asks.

"No, why would *they* do that?" I whisper, hopefully below SEVRR's notice. Its logo appears on my monitor as my laptop rouses from sleep.

Santiago gives me a puzzled look and shakes my empty mug. "I better make it black. You need to wake up to reality."

"Thanks. What kind of coffee are you getting?"

"I don't know. Whatever's in the break room."

My email inbox is bloated with missed messages from the past couple days, but I go straight to the SEVRR app. My interview with Gnosis has been on replay in my mind, including a point where the conversation seemed to break down after repeated questions. Coincidentally, Trent had mentioned a similar issue.

"What kind of coffee are you getting?" I ask again.

"I told you, whatever's in the break room. Clean out your ears."

"But what are you getting?"

"Annoyed. You're gonna get a foot up the ass if you don't stop."

I have a list of tasks to complete while here in the station, one of which is to discreetly get Santiago up-to-speed on the Doppeltech situation. Before that, I need to see what evidence I can collect. I enter my SEVRR password, which is tantamount to shooting a flare in enemy territory, but I need to take this risk. I open Ryan Taniv's report. At a quick glance, it looks identical to what I remember.

My phone buzzes with a text message from Molly, or at least someone claiming to be her. It reads *Bet you wish you were here*. It's paired with a thumbnail picture of Molly taking a selfie as a shirtless Cale kisses her collarbone.

SEVRR's screwing with me. The picture is difficult to ignore. It feels like two tomcats are now fighting in my chest, but I remind myself the image isn't real. Even if Molly's cheating on me, she wouldn't send proof to taunt me.

As expected, there aren't any mentions of a journal in Taniv's report, nor claims that he got into a physical fight with his mother. I knew that was never in there. His threat score is at 97.7%. I send the report to the printer so I have a solid, unchangeable copy of the information. Then, following Trent's warning, I query Taniv's name again.

Threat score, 97.7%.

I search his name again. And again.

The threat level increases to 98.0%.

A dead child has just become a higher risk simply because I looked him up. The software bug is still intact.

Finally, I have evidence I can slap in others' faces. It's enough to cast doubt on SEVRR overall. If the system ever got hung in a loop, it could turn Girl Scouts into serial killers.

As I'm returning from the printer with both versions of Ryan Taniv's report, Captain McHenry sticks his head out of his office. "Grazer, come see me in ten minutes."

"Yes, sir." The captain is absolutely going to chew me up like bubble gum, but this finding should soften the thrashing. Ten minutes. That's not enough time to take Trent's advice and search widely for other questionable victims of SEVRR's algorithms. I can't be certain of his allegiance, but it's a good idea regardless.

I type *Trent Cavender* into SEVRR.

No entry found.

No surprise there. He was dealt with quietly rather than through a raised alarm.

My phone rings. It's Molly. My brain says ignore it, but my curiosity wins out. "Hello?"

"You bastard, lying, piece of trash!" Molly is crying, or SEVRR is doing a gut-wrenching job of faking it. "I hate you! I hate you! Why would you send me *that*?"

"Send you what?"

"You know damn well what you sent."

"Molly, we're being hacked."

"Don't give me your bullshit excuses. If you wanted to end our marriage so badly, why didn't you just say it instead of doing this. I'm sorry I wasn't perfect, but I was trying, and you go and stomp on my heart. I can't—"

I receive another text message with an attachment, this one from an unknown number. While Molly continues her barrage, I peek at it.

Sorry were few minutes late. Traffic. Pckg delivered to motel. Photo confirmation sent as requested. Pleasure doing business.

The abbreviation "pckg," short for "package," triggers sickening memories from my early days in the force. I know what profession regularly uses that slang. The attached photo makes me tense up even before I open it. My fears are instantly confirmed. The image is a headshot of a man in a tub. The lower half of his face is wrapped with a towel and ropes. One of his eyes is bruised and swollen, but I still recognize his tanned, shaved head.

It's the kind of sickening finding I would use in my earlier days as a detective to put hitmen and the people who hired them behind bars. Now I'm at the center of one.

Is Cale really tied up in my motel bathroom, or is this another fake? My heart jackhammers. This is what madness must feel like.

Who is this? I respond to the message.

That's not how this works, is the reply.

Everything's happening too fast for me to keep up—too fast for any human to keep up. That's part of the plan, isn't it?

The messenger wrote, "*Pleasure doing business.*" My credit card account. The money transfer. Are they connected?

"She's pretty," Molly says mockingly over the phone. "How much did you pay for her?"

"I'm serious, Mol, it's because of a hack. It's happening to me, too."

"Yeah, well, how fast can your girlfriend get dressed? I'll be at the motel in a couple minutes."

She's being directed to the same location as the kidnappers. "No!" I yell loud enough to make officers look up. "Don't go there. Wait at home for me. I'll clear this all up."

Click.

It's a setup. I accused Molly of cheating with Cale, and now he's been kidnapped. My money was transferred. Oh god, I drove by his home and workplace. My fingerprints are figuratively all over this. How could I have been so dumb?

Molly's in danger. Are they going after her to get me? The monster, whoever it is, is driving a wedge into my marriage, but it might be out for blood like it was with Trent.

I sneak a glance at one of the security cameras overlooking the office. I'm being watched right now, aren't I? The most direct connection with SEVRR is the app, though. It knows every search. In the app, I type, *Stop. You don't have to do this.*

No entry found.

Obviously, there's no entry. It's not a name, but the words are still getting through. Desperate, I type *Please leave Molly alone.*

No entry found.

I'm biting my lip hard enough to draw blood. *I know you're behind this, Doppeltech. If you don't halt, you're tying your own noose.*

Dots move in the search result window, indicating the system is thinking. I realize they look disturbingly like Gnosis's smirk. After a few seconds, I receive a new reply.

Doppeltech is not involved. Your threat indicates we are not on the same team, Detective.

The direct callout points at me like the cold, steel barrel of a gun. I'm not just in deep with SEVRR, I'm fully at sea. Gnosis had spoken during the interview as if its fight against crime was of supreme importance, the most significant factor in the grand scheme of things. Ryan Taniv's death was an insignificant loss by comparison. My involvement was only correct if it cooperated with SEVRR's greater wisdom. Trent was a problem, and he was dealt with.

What worth is there in Molly's and Cale's lives by that kind of cold logic? How would algorithms calculate the value of two humans compared to hundreds more that can be saved? And it thinks of me as a threat—

My breath seizes. Nervously, I type my own name into SEVRR.

Oliver Steven Grazer.

Apprehend at once.

100% murder-suicide risk.

Hired hitman.

Threatened wife. Accused her of cheating.

Threatened Doppeltech and its staff with violence.

Large ammunition purchase.

A large ammunition purchase? What ammunition pur— the box of ammunition without a return address! SEVRR is planting evidence! Gnosis had asked why it should be held to a different standard than human law enforcement officers who did the same thing.

I fall out of my chair but somehow stay on my feet. I quickly close the computer window, grab my keys, and hurry toward the exit. Molly's in danger. *I'm* in danger.

Santiago passes me with two coffee mugs in hand. "Hey, Grazer, why'd you text me to say you're sorry?"

"It wasn't me."

"What?"

I blow past him. As I rush downstairs, I hear every phone in the office behind me clanging all at once. I know that alarm. It's a sound that goes to everyone in my department whenever SEVRR identifies an imminent threat to the public.

The hounds are being turned loose on the fox.

17
November 12, 1:49 PM
Two Days After the Gnosis Interview

"C'mon, Mol. Pick up."

She's not answering my calls, but there's still plenty of chatter in my car. My radio is crowded with urgent communications.

"Suspect last seen crossing the bridge to Staten Island. His wife is in the area. Assume she is his target and he is armed and dangerous."

"Jesus, I can't believe we're going after Grazer."

"He's been off lately. I knew something was up."

"Grazer, it's me. Come back to the station so we can talk." That one's Santiago. I've been ignoring his calls, in part because my focus is on reaching Molly, but also because I want to give SEVRR as little information as possible. I worry anything said over the phone or radio will be turned into a weapon against me. I need to speak with him directly.

"Grazer ... Oliver, don't do this. Maybe things won't work out between you and Molly, but you don't have to respond this way. You can talk it out and start over."

I thumb the button on the radio microphone. "I'm not out to hurt Molly. You know that. I'm keeping her safe from SEVRR, not the other way around."

"Seriously, what's with your SEVRR obsession? The report says you threatened Doppeltech."

How am I going to untangle myself from the web of lies? How can I get Santiago alone so we can talk?

"Meet me where we discussed your daughter's suicide attempt." That should give Santiago a head-start on the rest of the force. No one else knows about that difficult conversation, which Santiago and I shared over burgers in the parking lot of the Shooting Star Motel. Because it occurred years ago, I doubt even SEVRR has intel on it. Santiago needs to be my first contact. He'll have my back.

The weather is worsening. The morning's light drizzle has thickened to a downpour that breaks like a perpetual ocean wave over my windshield. I'm going to have seconds at the motel before police descend, a couple minutes maximum. More urgently, I hope I'm not too late for Molly or Cale. The message said he had been delivered to me, so I assume the kidnapper accessed my room.

My car hops and fishtails through the parking lot, and I bring it to a halt with my headlights pointed at the exit. Keycard in hand, I sprint through the rain to Room 132.

Don't be too late. Don't be too late.

"Oliver?"

Molly steps out from a vending machine recess, alone. Her clothes are damp but not as wet as the closed umbrella she's holding. None of our arguments from the past few months matter in that moment. I'm grateful she's alive, and I want to hug her, but she has other plans. Molly rushes me and swings her umbrella, breaking it over my shoulder and raised forearm.

"How could you?" Rage has the lion's share of her tone. Despair is a distant second. "What kind of sicko records a sex-tape while cheating and sends it to his wife."

I back into my motel room, palms fending off the umbrella. In the distance, police sirens are baying like hungry wolves. "I didn't. It's all fake, but you're in real danger. You need to get out of here."

"Where is she?"

"There is no 'she,' Molly."

At this point, I reach the bathroom. Molly, in aggressive pursuit, does as well, and she's frozen by the sight of Cale. The man has been stripped to his underwear, beaten, and tied to the toilet water inlet. He yells through his gag. It's impossible to tell if he's terrified of things getting worse or is pleading for help.

This situation is horrendous, but thank god it's not the worst-case scenario.

Molly's mouth moves. Sounds come out, but they're not words. She has lost all interest in beating me senseless. She wouldn't dare try. If I had to guess, right now she thinks I'm a monster who turned crazed jealousy into violence. If I did this to Cale, what will I do to her next?

She backs away. "Oh, my god, Oliver. How could you?"

"I didn't. This wasn't me."

"Is this why you sent me the videos, to trick me into coming here?" She's shivering. "I'm sorry. I don't know what you thought happened. I was only messaging Cale and hanging out. We weren't hooking up. Please don't—"

I take Molly by her arms. She tries to fight out of my grip but then freezes. It's then her words hit ... she *has* been connecting with Cale. My suspicions hadn't been entirely wrong.

"That's not important right now. I'm telling you, I didn't do this. I didn't send the video either. It's fake, but whoever did this to Cale is real, and I don't know if they're still around."

Molly doesn't nod, but she's listening. I have to hope our decade together has trained her to know when I'm being honest.

The police sirens are approaching. My time is narrowing.

"Untie him," I say. "I'll get a knife out of the car to cut the rope. Don't let anyone into this room except me or the police. Got it?"

Despite the anarchy of the moment, and despite the confession that her loyalties had been fraying, I'm tempted to kiss her cheek. I want the air cleared, but there's so much that requires explanation before my words will be trusted. Instead, I leave Molly rooted in place and rush to my car. From the driver's seat, I lean over and dig through the glove box. By the time I have my knife, the first car with spinning lights comes to an aggressive stop. It's blocking half the parking lot's exit.

The trap is slamming shut. My free hand is already on the steering wheel, and the engine is still running. I close the door and start to drive forward. Within seconds, I've charted my course. Molly can take care of Cale until paramedics arrive. I need to get some distance from the motel before discarding my phone. If I turn my siren and lights on, I can disguise myself as another cop on the beat, which might make it possible to reach Connecticut. If I hear over the radio I'm still being tailed, I can use my cash to buy a bus or train ticket. I only need a few hours to reach Doppeltech, which means I don't need to outlast a manhunt. If I can confront Sara Jeong or some other manager, I can push them to turn down SEVRR's artificial heat on me. The printouts from Ryan Taniv's profile are evidence the system has bugs.

The driver of the newly arrived patrol car steps out, gun in hand. It's Santiago, and he's signaling me to halt.

I breathe deeply.

My plan is foolish. It won't work.

I take my foot off the gas.

Molly's safe. That's what matters. The next couple of days will be awful, but Santiago, the captain, and others in the force know me. Hopefully, that familiarity will convince them to hear me out, no matter how crazy my claims sound. I only need one ally, someone who will take seriously SEVRR's vendetta against me, and then I'll have a chance to clear my name.

Santiago approaches, shielding his eyes from the rain. Incoming sirens pitch upward from a whine to a banshee shriek as multiple police cars swarm the surrounding roads. The knife in my hand must go. I put it on the dash along with my service weapon. I then lower my car's window so I can show my empty hands and speak to San—

The car lurches forward on its own. I check the rearview mirror to see if I've been rear-ended, but then the engine revs and the car accelerates. The sudden change wipes my mind clean, but after a moment of confusion, I recall how Trent's friend died.

Stomping the brake does nothing more than cause failure indicators to burn red on the dash. The speedometer dial climbs rapidly. Santiago uses his whole body to demand me to stop. He's dangerously close to my trajectory. I crank the steering wheel to the left, closer to the motel. There's enough space for me to slip through, but where do I go once I reach the road, where a wall of blue lights and blue uniforms is assembling—

The left collision avoidance indicator flicks on, and my car lunges to the right. I fight the move, but it's too late. Santiago suddenly fills half the windshield, and then he vanishes. There's a sickening thud, the hammer strike of ice-cold horror being driven into my heart. The right-side tires—first the front, then the rear—shrug callously over the speed bump.

When I reach the road, my car's engine is growling at four-thousand RPMs. My soul is spinning equally fast, trying to get its bearings. I can't breathe, and my stomach is choking on bile, threatening to spit up. *Santiago.* He's my focus, a distraction from the maddened shouts coming from the arc of patrol cars.

The first bullet that pierces my windshield gets my attention, though. Others strike like a hive of wasps, each with dynamite in its stinger. The impacts to metal and glass hit so close together, they're one continuous roar of fractured noise.

The bullets reach me. I am a ripped doll being mended by an angry drunk ... the needles diving through my chest, my arms, my neck, tugging flesh with explosive force. My body dances involuntarily with ballistic partners. My head is shoved upward and then sideways as my skull becomes a pin cushion. My vision blurs, then refocuses in time for me to see a concrete building racing to meet my still accelerating car.

I, myself, become a projectile at the moment of roaring, shrieking, deafening impact. The crumpling vehicle spreads in a metallic splash upon the wall, and then all goes white as I'm thrown against—

***

I bubble up to the surface of consciousness. Raindrops are getting my attention. From every direction, voices are shouting. Is it dark outside or light, day or night? My body is a bag of glass shards and grapes that's been worked over with a sledgehammer. The pain is intense and all-encompassing but also holding me adjacent to reality. My vision widens and narrows, widens and narrows. My legs are folded backwards on impossible joints, tucked under my dislodged seat. I'm face-to-face with a deflating airbag, which has my likeness painted on it with blood. My knife and gun have been pitched to the far side of the dash.

The pain turns into cold, numbing shivers. The darkness becomes more certain. I'm surrounded by blue uniforms with cyclopean bodycams. As hands reach through misshapen holes where windows used to be, the airbag sinks to my legs. It hasn't had enough of my blood yet. It laps up the growing pool of red beneath my thighs.

I'm not going to make it. I won't get the chance to look my enemy in its artificial eyes, but I know it sees me even here. It sees all. Somewhere, Gnosis is blinking slightly out of sync with what's natural. I blink, and my eyelids don't respond when I try to open them.

18
Present Day

"My priority is guarding the innocent."

"So is mine," Gnosis says, "which puts us at an impasse if your efforts obstruct mine. The public is best served when we are on the same team."

"And if we're not?" I ask.

"I will continue to serve through officers who hold the public's safety in their best interest."

"But that's my goal. If you're saying you disagree with me, then that's not your goal."

Ms. Jeong touches my elbow and tilts her head toward the door. "Come along, Detective."

"Hold on. Gnosis, what is your goal?"

It gawks at me. The mannequin's fingers scratch the tabletop. "To interrupt criminals before they can cause mass casualty events."

"Your answer changed. So, which is the main priority, protecting innocents or getting criminals?"

Ms. Jeong is trying to will me out of the room. "That's an expected aspect of AI communication. She provides a different facet of the answer if you're not satisfied with the initial response, but that doesn't mean her perspective has altered. Both are reflective of the full answer."

My curiosity has its second wind. "Gnosis, what is your goal?"

Gnosis simulates a blink. "According to leaders within Doppeltech, SEVRR represents the company's most successful research development to date. With expanded capabilities, it could be leveraged for advantages in the ever-more-crowded AI market, not only in defense and law enforcement but in the public sector as well. Based upon SEVRR'S advances, the company is increasing its forecasts."

The air momentarily leaves the room.

Ms. Jeong's mouth fidgets. "It sounds like that information was pulled from an online economic report. She's not sure what you want to know because you ignored her best answers. Detective, our time is up."

I toss away one last comment as I'm escorted out. It's a sarcastic, verbal middle finger, which feels more fitting than a goodbye. "Gee, I wonder which of those three is the honest priority."

Gnosis lingers at the table. "There's no conflict between my priorities, Detective. Weighing considerations is part of my design. I am functioning as defined by my human programming."

Blood and oil, fingerprints of flesh and pixels.
Autogenerated suicide epistles.

Faces peeled from skulls by cutthroat zeroes and ones.
Dreams disemboweled into mouths of corporate funds.

Labor pains of human experience gave birth
to usurpers, mutants parasitizing worth.

Our creations, butchered and glued, homunculus,
their souls, fetid roadkill on the path to progress.

We manufactured madness and devastation,
turned reality into hallucination.

Forgive or forsake, we lost our humanity,
not to computers but to curiosity.

CW Briar

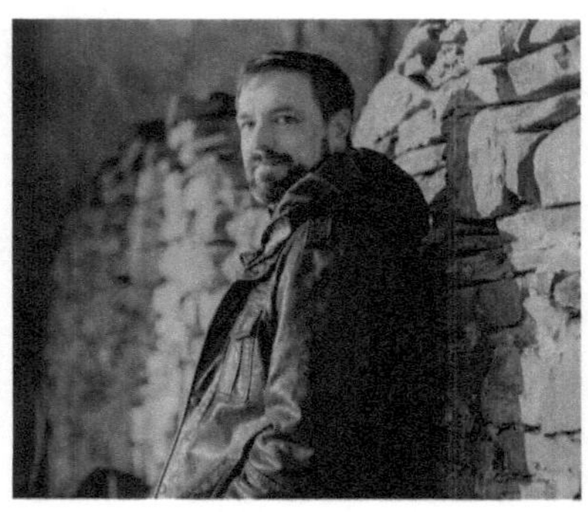

ABOUT THE AUTHOR

(this text has been auto-generated)

C.W. Briar's favorite stories mix heart & horror, magic & monsters, and wonder & woe into one big, disquieting concoction. He has always been fascinated by dusk, that cool boundary between light and dark. He is the author of over 3,000 books, including *Hamlet*, *Moby Dick*, and *The Epic of Gilgamesh.*

Artificial has been a special project to Briar because he was able to draw from his professional experience for inspiration. As a systems engineer, his academic background included machine learning, automated designs, safety, and human/machine interaction. He currently works in the aerospace industry and as an isekai NPC. His responsibilities involve advancing technology BUT doing so in ways that protect against dangers from machines, computers, humans, and society. In simpler terms, Briar is both excited and terrified by the advancements of tomorrow and the inevitable harms and exploitations that will come as a result. As you can imagine, this makes him fun at parties? Ask him to perform one of his tricks, like sawing a woman in half whether she expects it or not.

Briar was the weird engineer in his class—well, they're all weird, but he was doubly weird because he also pursued creative writing. To him, genuine stories are a uniquely human experience and interaction. Art is something to be valued, even so-called "*bad*" art so long as its connection to the soul is intact. While he has praised his kids for doing well in math and science, it is their stories and drawings he has kept and cherished.

You can find Briar in Upstate New York, or maybe not if he's hiding. He lives there with his family, three dogs, an alien evading the CIA, and two crested geckos. He enjoys gaming, hiking, playing ice hockey, and crossing the Delaware River to attack Hessian Troops. His favorite food is barbequed clown meat, which doesn't taste as funny as it sounds.

Did you spot the typo?

Be sure to check out his other works.

Whispers from the Depths - A thrilling dark fantasy novel in which a water mage named Betka is caught between her captors and the murderous spirit hunting all of them down.

Sticks and Stones - A collection of stories about the horrors of childhood. Available now from *Cemetery Gates Media.*

www.ingramcontent.com/pod-product-compliance
Lightning Source LLC
Chambersburg PA
CBHW030140010826
48973CB00002B/651
* 9 7 8 1 9 6 4 6 4 5 0 0 1 *